TARGET

Stand by for **The Bronze Heist** – and Steve Hackett's toughest case to date

GW01605778

There were t … with arms floating … he sun was shining ar … world occupied every … wasn't interested in the statue. N … aluzzi. Hackett could see him, hiding behind the boat with a Luger in his fist. Hackett was crouched in cover too, but he would have to get closer soon, he would have to take the risk and break cover. Paluzzi, like a wraith in sunlight, was beginning to fade. It was now or never. With a supreme effort of will, his whole body screaming at him to stop, Hackett dashed out of hiding and ran towards Paluzzi. He pulled his gun up. His body was trembling. Paluzzi was aiming his Luger. Hackett could see the glisten of oil on the gun and of pomade in his hair. Paluzzi fired. . . .

TARGET

The Bronze Heist

Michael Feeney Callan

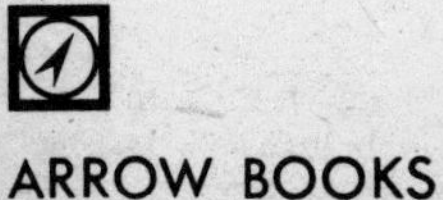

ARROW BOOKS

To Cecily and to A. and K.

Arrow Books Ltd
3 Fitzroy Square, London W1P 6JD

An imprint of the Hutchinson Publishing Group

London Melbourne Sydney Auckland Wellington Johannesburg and agencies throughout the world

First published 1978
Arrow edition 1978
© Michael Feeney Callan 1978

This book is sold subject to the condition that it shall not, by way of trade or otherwise, be lent, resold, hired out, or otherwise circulated without the publisher's prior consent in any form of binding or cover other than that in which it is published and without a similar condition including this condition being imposed on the subsequent purchaser.

Set in 10 on 12 Press Roman by BSC Graphics Ltd, London

Made and printed in Great Britain by The Anchor Press Ltd, Tiptree, Essex

ISBN 0 09 918990 9

The characters and settings in this book are based on those in the BBC TV series *Target*, produced by Philip Hinchcliffe and starring Patrick Mower and Brendan Price.

1

There are moments in every involved and protracted job, Hackett thought grimly, when alertness diminishes and the brain changes gear and devolves to an inner automatic computer. The efficiency of that computer you do not question: if it has been good enough to allow you to maintain your rank, then it *is* good enough. But, like the car you drive, you trust it with reserved suspicion and you always wish it could be that little much better. When the moment comes you switch over to it with a degree of unwillingness.

Hackett was tired, blindingly tired. In the last twenty-four hours he had covered vast mileage in no less than three countries in pursuit of a target criminal, an organiser of illegal immigration who had been evading police nets continually for four years. Information from the Bunderskriminalampt in Frankfurt had come through to the effect that the man had based himself in Wiesbaden and that a large-scale operation from a French port was in preparation. Hackett, in company of Detective Inspector Grant and Woman Detective Sergeant Louise Colbert, had flown to Frankfurt and taken up the trail from the *Gasthaus* where the man was known to work from. But they had missed him in Wiesbaden; and in Mechelen; and finally the job had blown-out stupidly in Calais. Grant had been recognised and the organisor had made a run for it. They had suspected he was making a dash for the Hoverport or docks and had covered there as best they could, but the man had side-stepped, taking a train for Paris at the station near the docks, and they had lost him completely. The smuggling operation had been short-circuited but nothing worthwhile had really been achieved. If anything, the organiser had gained from the exercise, learning for sure now that the Squad was after him and was prepared to spend money to take him in. He would be more cautious about his safe house in future, and the task for Hackett would be all the harder. And so too would be Hackett's resolve. Before leaving Calais he had drafted in another man to replace Grant and despatched him and Louise to Paris to take up any possible leads there. Then, on specific request of his Co-ordinator, Chief Superintendent Tate, he had flown home, with the disfavoured Grant.

They had touched down not two hours ago, breakfasted at the airport, then split up – Grant to return to a warm bed and a warm wife, Hackett to snatch twenty minutes of shut-eye in his office chair before poring over the memoranda and notes that invariably accumulated during the briefest of absences. There had been nothing spectacular: a note from MPD about operations of Squad men in their territory; a couple of CROs Hackett had been looking for a week ago; a C-11 reply to his query about dropped charges on a small-time hood; a belated Interpol report on the immigrant-smuggler's cover in France; a clipping someone had thoughtfully pulled from the *Evening News* relating to a long-running current target job . . .

Hackett read carefully through the lot, filed the CROs in his own cabinet, then shaved and had a coffee – his tenth since midnight – from the corridor machine. He was knocking back the dredges when the telephone buzzed. It was nine o'clock and the girl's voice was depressingly cheerful and lively. She informed him that Chief Superintendent Tate was waiting in his office and that the Assistant Chief Constable (Operations) had now arrived. The meeting would commence in fifteen minutes. Hackett crossed to the window and lifted it wide open. He screwed his eyes closed, feeling the sting of sleep burning through the sockets, and breathed deeply a dozen times. This meeting with the ACC was important and he wanted to get the best from it. The facts to be conveyed were not the top consideration – these could always be studied later from the departmental planning reports; but Hackett was anxious to observe keenly the interaction of the various involved parties. Harmony was the prime requisite in a tight co-ordinated plan like the one at hand and at these late stages it was vital to sort out the obstructive from the imaginative and choose your allies.

Reporting briefly to Tate (who ignored his bleary-eyed, uncommunicative state), both men then went through to the assigned meeting room on the third floor. There, six quietly-dressed, relaxed-looking men were gathered round an oversize desk. Hackett recognised all but one of the men, a rotund tough character with a Joe Louis-type face and a powder-blue suit that seemed as incongruous in the dull room as a peacock feather in a military cap. This newcomer was seated behind the desk with the ACC, whose towering bulk dwarfed everyone.

Opposite, Pemberton of the Force Special Branch sat between Chief Superintendent Shaw and a sour-faced little man called Burgess from Intelligence. Slouched in a chair at the top of the desk, at right angles to everyone else, sat Havelock, a man of deceptive abstraction and lazy expressions. Now, as Hackett sank into a chair beside Shaw, Havelock's hooded eyes drifted coolly to him, blinked unhappy recognition and sidled off. Tate brusquely apologised to the ACC for their late arrival. The ACC waved the remark aside and bluntly introduced the blue-suited man as a secretary from the American Embassy in Grosvenor Square.

'This informal meeting is by way of final confirmation,' the ACC went on. 'Yesterday, as you know, we had a get-together with the Legal Attaché at the Embassy who is acting as liaison between ourselves and the Washington people. The possibility of the cancellation of the State Visit has now been cleared up. Everything is settled and we have a definite green light.'

Hackett saw Tate sigh and Shaw move restlessly in his chair. He could imagine what they were thinking – just exactly what he was thinking. The forthcoming visit of the American President would be a prestige event for the two countries, a source of enjoyment and entertainment for the thousands who would line the routes and wave the flags – and a thorn in the side for policemen of every rank in the Met and the divisions. Leave would be cancelled, duty rosters would be turned upside-down, territorial boundaries would be argued over and all the friction and farce of close co-operative work between the Branch and the Squad and Uniform and Intelligence would erupt into calculated warfare. Hopes had been high for a full week that the event might be postponed because of mounting conflict on the Russo-Chinese border, but that was settled now: the circus was on the road.

'Without repeating all we've already discussed,' the ACC said, 'I'll reiterate for our American friend here: Shaw is in charge of traffic and route planning for the visit . . . .' The American grinned to Shaw. 'Burgess is from Criminal Intelligence and is working closely with the State Department people and the US Secret Service . . . .' Burgess' arch look avoided the American's smile. 'Detective Chief Inspector Pemberton is, of course, from Force Special Branch and will be working in close association with Chief Superintendent Tate and Superintendent Hackett of the Regional Crime Squad.' Hackett saw Tate frown thoughtfully. Always a man for precision, the generality of the ACC's reference would annoy Tate, he knew. As yet, the squad's position had not been defined but this link with the branch was more or less expected. Hackett guessed that in hard terms it would mean a rather loose working friendship. The squad would not participate in Special Branch work and would be solely occupied with surveillance and checking-up on known criminals and militant anarchist or communist groups. On the day, Hackett's job would be the deployment of Authorised Shots from the Squad's crack team. These men would line the President's route through the city, placed at danger spots and armed with high-power Parker Hale rifles. Now, with the go-ahead for the visit, Hackett would have to draw up his own Operational Plan and the next few days would offer little rest from intensive desk and street work. Extra work would be loaded on every squad man and woman. There were a half-dozen target operations of one sort or another in advanced stages at present and the President job would just mean one more – heavier – deadweight. Another file, a new card index . . . .

Hackett pulled himself from a rambling reverie to listen to the ACC.

'Detective Chief Superintendent Havelock here is Head of CID and will, for operational purposes, be in charge of the entire set-up. The Force Operations Room on the second floor will be the central base for all our planning and execution.' The ACC paused to light a pipe and gauge the American's reaction. The fat man smiled – a smile that seemed to evince total non-comprehension, to Hackett's eye. The ACC ignored the lame look and stared at Havelock. 'Can I ask you to comment on immediate requirements?'

'All the obvious things,' Havelock replied in his dry, laconic voice. 'Full assistance from the FBI men in the Embassy and our boys in the Met. Work-wise we're well ahead and I don't foresee any problems. The Operations Room is monitoring everything but big crime is unlikely during the trip. The pros know when to keep out of the city. Too much police activity. Small stuff – pick-pockets, hawkers – that'll be looked after at uniform level. I'll speak to Deane about that. The other major consideration is the lunatic fringe, the danger to the President. There's always that worry.'

Silence.

Eyes edged across to Pemberton, willing response. But Pemberton was lost to concentration, head down, scribbling furiously on a sheet of police stationery.

'Have you anything particularly in mind for the Squad?' Tate put in. 'We'd prefer a finite task. It always helps to know where boundaries begin and end.'

Havelock shrugged. 'Preventive medicine at the moment. You know yourself. Find out who's in the city just now. Scratch around. Make sure our old friends are keeping quiet. If any specific intelligence comes from Burgess here, or from the FBI – or the Police Judiciaire for that matter – if anything nasty shows, you're first on the job. After that we'll want your firing power. How many Shots have you got?'

Tate looked to Hackett. The jaded computer in the back of Hackett's head shuddered into action. Stirring the memory bank was momentarily almost painful. 'Twenty-one.'

'How many will we need?' the ACC asked.

The question was directed to Havelock but Pemberton took it. 'In general terms, we'll need all we can get – so Hackett's boys will be welcome. We have worked out a placings map but we'll want to go over the final route when Shaw and the Americans have agreed on it – and I take it that's just about done?'

The ACC nodded through a spiral of smoke and turned back to the American. 'Right then, we're ready to go, it seems. Perhaps you'd give us a final word about the President's plans?'

The fat boxer's face fractured into a network of lines,

forming a cordial, PR countenance as the man started talking in a turgid, Mid-West drawl. Hackett's brain clicked off again and allowed the facts to tread through the computer. From the tail of his eye he saw Tate scowl at him and he realised vaguely that his head was lolling like a drunken man's on the back of his chair: only then did the incongruity of his appearance strike him. He hadn't looked in a mirror for thirty hours and the clothes he wore – a dark suede jacket and two-year-old jeans – were crumpled and scuffed. He could smell his own sweat and he hadn't bothered to comb his hair when he'd rushed that shave. In contrast, the men who sat around him, fresh from bed and meals, were neat, clean and groomed. It was little wonder the American's eyes returned again and again to him as he talked.

'. . . Originally we felt the Downing Street talks would be as much as the President could manage, but he was eager to extend the visit if at all possible because, as well as everything else, he has strong family ties – as you all know – with this part of the country. The proposal was then made for a stop-off trip here and the university kindly invited the President to perform the opening ceremony of the new wing.'

'He arrives by helicopter?'

'Right. There are no changes to our original arrangements. He touches down at Royal Pier. The itinerary, briefly, then reads: procession route through city – thirty minutes motor run; the university, where there will be speeches with the deans of faculties and president – no more than thirty minutes' duration; then it's on to City Hall for luncheon – approximately two hours; and then a walkabout of about one hour. And departure from Royal Pier.'

'The walkabout will create our greatest problems,' Pemberton commented unhappily. 'I've already conveyed this to the Legal Attaché.'

'The President is keen to make contact with people,' the American said. 'The whole purpose of the journey here is to meet the townsfolk. He is mindful of the difficulties but thinks it would be easier to do this sort of thing here than in London.'

But not for us, Hackett thought wryly. With a walk-about the risks were always monstrous. Security men on the ground and long-distance sharp-shooters were taxed to their fullest. The margins of error broadened enormously and it became virtually impossible to provide adequate cover; but the task of trying to plug the gaps would fall on Pemberton and Hackett. An elaborate arrangement of Shots would have to be set up, Hackett reflected, and, though Pemberton had probably already prepared it using hypothetical figures, a man-for-man plan would have to be drafted as soon as possible. When the complexity of that sort of preparation hit Hackett he shrugged the entire notion off instantly. *That* sort of thinking would have to be done on another day, with a fresher mind. Because, at that stage, there would be no room for exhausted miscalculations.

'I've had no answer from my telex to Grosvenor Square about threats on the President's life,' Burgess said suddenly, his powerful, barracks-square voice overriding the American in mid-sentence. 'I hope the President's Security people are going to be helpful. We can't work out on a limb. And time is getting tight.' He stopped swiftly, savage accusation in the full stop. The fat American smiled equably. 'Of course the FBI will help as best we can. But you'll appreciate we're inordinately busy at the Embassy. You'll allow for that.'

'We're concerned with every possible source of danger being countered,' Burgess came back. 'We've been told Washington gets up to six threats a week. We will need details that might affect us. Anything substantial, anything that may carry over here.' He hesitated, coughed. 'After all, Intelligence work is the back-bone of this kind of event.'

Havelock cringed and grimaced in annoyance and the ACC puffed heavily on his pipe. Hackett smiled inwardly. Burgess never failed to connect. And irritate. It was, Hackett suspected, a practiced device to deter would-be 'mates' from other departments who might undervalue his work and expect more than the standard quota of information in exchange for their friendliness. Hackett didn't know Burgess to have one friend; but he had plenty of admirers. And the system was always the same, this blistering openness.

'Do you, in fact, anticipate an attempt on his life?' The American's question was thinly veiled sarcasm. Even Hackett was awake enough to detect that. But the nuance apparently skipped over Burgess' head. For the first time he smiled slightly, satisfied at reaction.

'I don't know. Right now I wouldn't even guess. I suppose there's always someone who'd like to have a crack at the man. A lot who'd do it for glory and a lot who'd do it for cash. It's up to your people to point us in the right direction. We collate and disseminate. It's up to your men to get out in the streets and pick up clues. We rely on the front line men. On the FBI. And the likes of Hackett's Squad . . . .'

'You're getting pretty transparent, you know.'

'How d'you mean?'

Tate made a bad effort at concealing a good-humoured smile. 'You sat in there like a lofty bloody pop star, not opening your mouth, staring at everyone like curios in museums.'

The ACC's meeting had dragged on for a full two hours

and, on conclusion, Hackett and Tate had spent a further ten minutes being briefed by Pemberton on the existing preparations of the Branch. Now, back in Tate's office, Hackett was commencing a full account of the blow-out in France. He stopped in his tracks and pulled a face. He was too tired to care about being diplomatic. 'Burgess gets to be a pain in the arse and Havelock yawns his way through everything. Makes as if it's a picnic outing.' He grinned. 'I suppose I was studying form in there.'

'What's your reading of the situation?'

'Well, we've no defined work as such within the planning, so I'll just sally on with what I'm at. I'll put a few men on the militant groups, sound out their movements. And I'll get heads together with Pemberton on individual cases, and preparing distribution of men for firing power on the day. That'll be our real job. I'll have to consult Havelock on that, find out exactly what he wants. Since we've just three days left, the sooner the better some of this gets done, I'll see Havelock before I leave . . .'

'Leave?'

'To get some kip. The red-rimmed eyes have nothing to do with wine, women and song.'

Tate considered Hackett's view of the prospects for a minute. A quick flicker of admiration for the duality of Hackett's personality lit in his mind. It was little wonder that the man, despite his comparative youth, had four distinguished, if controversial, years behind him as Superintendent in Charge of Operations. In a world of wild cats he was a Bengal Tiger – a tough man who thrived on excitement and challenge and yet possessed the subtlety of imagination and sagacity. His assimilative powers never dulled and he had the capacity to make big jobs look puny. In the field he was a fearless, formidable man and behind a desk, in Tate's view, he was no less impressive. One day, with the brittle edge chipped off him and some of the impetuousness deflated, he would make a sterling Co-ordinator.

'That's as I see it,' Tate said at last. 'Top consideration from our point of view is movement of our known friends.' He stood up and ambled over to the wall cabinet. 'I don't want any loose ends hanging round – not now. If anything crazy is going to happen, it's not going to happen here.'

'Yeah. I get the gist. America's Golden Boy can hit the deck anywhere but in our territory.'

Tate shot a black, reproachful look. He pushed a folder with a C-11 stamp on the front to Hackett. 'I wanted you back specifically to sound this out. You won't thank Burgess for it, but he was the one who came up with it. Came to me yesterday, wanted to know if we were onto it.'

Hackett sifted through the material in the folder. There were four or five photostats of Yard documents, a D/F complete with photograph and a few scant notes in Tate's distinctive handwriting. The CRO listing the man's record was a wordy treatise. Hackett glanced at the name – Richard Freeman Gifford – and for a second it didn't register. He scanned the background details and the character – and the case – came back to him quickly. An East End upbringing, Gifford had started dabbling in petty crime at an early age. Convictions ranged from demanding with menace to assault and the first recorded was dated over twenty-five years ago. There was an addendum to the record card which was headed 'Activities 1962-'63' and gave scant account of mercenary work in Central Africa, believed involvement in arms smuggling and an association with an assassination attempt on a black leader. The CRO showed no convictions for '64-'65 but Gifford must have been conserving energies, because the following year, 1966, was the time of the Big One. It was unnecessary to re-read the details. Hackett recalled. He had been a Divisional Detective Sergeant at the time and the case had meant overtime for everyone in the Force. A German businessman, head of a multi-national company supplying cash and equipment for Britain's early space programme, had been kidnapped from his hotel in High Wycombe. The kidnapping and subsequent ransom plot were carried out with a superb military precision which had given the Yard its first lead. The forensic boys had turned up nothing and, though just about every known villain capable of that kind of crime was interviewed – including Gifford – not one break into the team was unearthed. Alibis were water-tight and the police had been continually misled, pursuing various channels. The multi-national corporation eventually paid the ransom and the team out-foxed every CID trick to take the haul and skip off. Gifford and his four friends took £200,000, and the businessman was released. The team went to Europe and enjoyed three months of freedom and high living but the tactics of the whole affair had already brought one man, James Robertson, under suspicion. When the CID called, Robertson's mother told them her son had absconded and had gone, she believed, to work as a mercenary soldier in Africa. Taking Robertson's record into account, this story was credible, but the Super in charge of the case still held him as prime suspect for leading the team. The breakthrough came a month later. A small-time hood who had acted as driver for the team during the kidnap job was arrested in South London for receiving – a charge totally unrelated to the big job. To save himself he grassed and the full story emerged: Robertson, Gifford and three other ambitious hoods were named. A case was prepared but pictures and names were not released to the newspapers. The following month Gifford and a man called Abney were arrested re-entering Britain and, before the year was out, each of the others had been lured home and taken in. The men had been, for a time, almost celebrities and when the final story of the crime and escape made the media headlines the ingenuity and panache of the villains gave rise to a kind of vindicating applause. But they went on to receive heavy sentences – Gifford (if Hackett remembered correctly) getting off lightest with twelve years. He had been released, Hackett saw from the CRO card, two years ago and no further convictions had been run up. Tate had written an address on a sheet of paper – in Hammersmith.

Hackett looked up. 'He's in town?'

'Staying at digs up on the Common. Address is there.'

'Hammersmith?'

'No. That's the family. His mother. He's been living there since his release. Uniform found him here. Street fight on Monday night. It could easily have slipped by but Burgess took it.'

'What did Havelock have to say?'

'Left it with me. He's not perturbed. Nothing too unusual about it.'

'Except that Gifford's a long way from home.'

'Wasn't his mate Abney born here?' Tate drummed his fingers on the desk, concentrating. 'I'll check up on that – there might be a link.'

'No harm checking up on them all – the Big Five. I'll put a telex up, see what we can get. They've all finished 'bird', I take it?' Tate nodded. 'Well – ' Hackett closed the file and stretched in his chair. 'Nothing like the personal touch. I'll drive out this evening and see if I can run him down, have a chat.' He frowned. 'But I can't see any possible connection with this American thing. I'd say Gifford's very happy to keep his nose clean after ten years inside.'

Tate pursed his lips, a mannerism of deep thinking. 'What really got me thinking was word from C-11 yesterday that Paluzzi is back.'

It was like a dousing in iced water. Since the airport, since the beginning of the ACC's meeting, Hackett had been functioning on reserve systems. His heart and his mind had been beating slower and the inner relaxation of muscles, that benumbed limbo before the discomfort of total exhaustion, had had him feeling pleasantly content. Now with the touch of a feather, the mention of a name, his nervous system jarred and crashed him into full alertness. A visual image to match the name tripped through his brain. Paluzzi – a slick grey-haired man with large black unnerving eyes, like fish-eyes, and a gentle demeanour. A large calm man who kept his hands in his coat pockets and always smiled at you like a dentist smiles to a patient. Hackett had only come face-to-face with the man once, and once had been enough. The image was indelibly scored on his mind.

'Where?' Hackett's voice was a half-shout that Tate understood and ignored.

'London. Fairly reliable say-so. Ex-Flying Squad man says he saw him in a West End club. Hair blackened, otherwise as ever.'

'Was there a follow? Did anyone try to make contact?'

'Fell apart. The Squad man tailed him, tried to get to a phone. Lost him.'

'Stupid . . .' Hackett was up and pacing. Digits, figures, dates, names, contacts rolled through his head. He had a hefty file on Paluzzi, he could check that. There was a Frenchman who ran a shipping agency – *he* knew him . . . If he dug deep enough there'd be plenty who knew him. By Christ there would! He'd had enough good runs here to make a score of friends and enemies. Someone would want to grass this time, someone would stab him in the back. Hackett cursed out loud. This time, by God – this time he'd take Paluzzi.

Tate said: 'They're keeping a fast eye out for him in the Met. But you know him, he might move, could show up anywhere. It could mean nothing but the coincidence of

Gifford showing up here and then hearing *he* was around – I just didn't like it.' Hackett took the point. Five years ago speculation had started suggesting that Paluzzi had been the ringleader of the Big Five's kidnap job. Substantial evidence had been amassed by a top-selling novelist who had spent years researching and, though the author was killed in rather questionable circumstances before the book saw the light of day, the published facts indicated a tenuous but vital link between Robertson, the team's leader, and Paluzzi. The facts created little stir outside the police force and by then Paluzzi was already known to intelligence and wanted for questioning in connection with a half-dozen other cases but the book represented the most solid documented account of a connection between Paluzzi and the underworld in Britain.

His back to Tate, staring out of the window, Hackett suddenly spoke in a measured, vicious monotone. 'Let that bastard cross into my camp and I'll nail him to the bloody wall. We owe him one.' His voice dropped to a whisper, became smug. 'I just hope he's planning a bloody hit.'

'But on what?' Tate said, almost uninterestedly. 'On who?'

Everything about Francisco Paluzzi seemed to belie the notoriety attached in some quarters to his name. He dressed inconspicuously, like a New York or London businessman, choosing dark blues and blacks rather than the mid-shades more popular in the country of his birth. His square handsome face was remarkable only in the regularity of its features and the youthful translucence of the skin. The oversize eyes and the slight turn-up at the corners of his mouth lent him a warm, sympathetic expression and his permanent manner seemed gentle and sincere. Outwardly, to the casual observer, he seemed a docile, simple man but the camouflage was God-given rather than affected and it concealed a seething personality that was intense, fanatical and touched with criminal genius.

Paluzzi's life of crime had begun on the back-streets of Naples, parading with roving bands of teenage *delinguenti* during the war years of American occupation. As a homeless gypsy he had earned more than a living stealing from GIs and from American Base Headquarters and touting for prostitutes in the docks. The immediate post-war years enabled him to continue his professional career manipulating black market goods and the step into dope peddling was a small one. He had started a pharmaceutical company in Florence and used it as a cover for importing dope from Tangier and Macao. There were richer pickings in America in the early fifties and Paluzzi was attracted by the million-dollar-a-week market on New York's streets. Mafia connections opened the door for him and in a matter of two years, by various devious methods, he had rocketed through the hierarchical structure and taken control of a vast gang specialising in narcotics smuggling to all the major US cities.

But Paluzzi wasn't a team worker. He was independent-minded and contrary. He didn't acknowledge any ground rules or follow any codes other than the ones that felt right at any given moment. He made enemies in New York, and Vegas, and Miami – and an inevitable gang war ran him from the States eventually, hounded by the Mafia's strong-arm boys and under threat of death. Paluzzi ran to cover but didn't stay put for long. Under an assortment of guises he started back in business – first in dope again, then graduating to diamonds, then arms. His reputation in the underworld not only in Italy but in Germany, France and the Baltic countries, soared and by tacit agreement the Mafia feud was stopped. Paluzzi was too big a nob, and too dangerous. He was influential, even in the legitimate business areas, and purportedly politically well placed. The

Mafia, in their generosity, gave him a clean bill and Europe was his.

For ten years everything rattled profitably along until, putting trust in the wrong bedmate, Paluzzi got framed for trafficking and the first significant conviction was chalked against him. A doldrums period began and a succession of carefully set plans fell down – from business investments to kidnap ventures, like the Big Five's hit, in which his £90,000 share for financing and planning was swindled from him.

In search of new pastures he moved to Britain, but his six-month stay there was no happier. The gun run he had mounted from Cuxhaven to supply terrorist groups in the city and in Northern Ireland failed and he had only managed to resist capture and arrest by shooting his way out of the port and fleeing the country. He had based himself in Berne with (he liked to tell himself) half the other criminals on the run in the world and taken a sabbatical.

He had never attempted to go back to Britain (or Italy for that matter, where he was still a wanted man), but had always relished the thoughts of a triumphal return – namely a worthy and successful 'pull'.

And now the time had come. An ambition of five years was about to be fulfilled and he was back in Britain to fulfil it.

For a wandering moment, as he pressed the metal button that fed air into his car tyres, he wondered if word had got out yet that he was back. He suspected it probably had and knew, like all operatives worth their metal, that from now on he would have to watch every move he made. It was more than a simple matter of vigilance. He would have to *assume* they were on to him. He thought about the girl, stood up and looked across the roof of the Mercedes towards the gaily-lit club with a high legend, *The Golden Gun*, surrounded by bubbles of neon. He glanced at his watch. The extra caution would even have to run as far as her. He had spoken to her on the phone at twelve, suggesting a meet at seven. Now it was six, and he had had the club under view for over an hour. First from the window of the café opposite, then on foot and by casual motoring round. The trouble was worth the feeling of security. No coppers had shown, nothing even slightly out of the ordinary, nothing to alert his trained eye.

Without further hesitation and leaving the car parked in the lot of the closed garage, Paluzzi crossed the wide street and entered the club. In the hallway entrance a wooden sign directed patrons through a curtained glass door. A second door at the back of the hall was marked 'Private'. Paluzzi walked across to this door and pressed the bell. The intercom sang and a plastic voice said, 'What is it?'

Paluzzi replied, 'Bryant.'

The door slid open. He walked quickly in and followed the stairs. There was a heady mixed smell of Chanel, alcohol and the hot flesh of animals. It was what he expected, what he wanted: the scent of sole occupancy. Despite the reassurances, on the landing he hesitated and checked each of the three rooms that lay in darkness. Then he moved into the livingroom. A fat Dobermann Pinscher reposing on the settee jerked excitedly up, recognised the visitor as familiar and non-playful, and sank back to slumber. The girl strode out from behind a partitioning curtain, a loose gown around her shoulders and her face half made-up. In her hands she carried glasses of Chianti. Paluzzi took his and made an inept remark about the suitability of the drink. Her sardonic reply, in a Bow Bells accent, was, 'Cheers!'

He sat with his drink while she whipped back the curtain and took position at the dressing-table. He watched her face in the mirror and thought, for the tenth time, how much facially and in personality she had changed from the frivolous fledgling of six years ago who had shared his bed. The humour had vanished from her pretty face and the lush black hair was trimmed now, and tinted a lack-lustre auburn. In conversation she was less compromising, far more arrogant and she cherished opinions like rich possessions and spoke loudly and decidedly on every topic under the sun. Where once she had been shy and sensitive, she was now imperious and sharp. But there was an artificiality in her that attracted Paluzzi still. In deep conversation her Italian lilt returned and she still wore the moonstone he'd given her all those years ago. Serena was, he guessed, a good actress who took pains to conceal her vulnerability.

'You expected me,' he said.

'Saw you coming. At the garage.' She smeared scarlet lipstick on, pulled her face back from the mirror and examined herself. Suddenly she smiled. The sensuousness of the change of expression, the memory of her old humour, made Paluzzi's heart race. He wished she would smile more.

'I have to be careful,' he said. 'I made mistakes before with the ladies in my life.' He softened that with a laugh. Serena didn't take it up. She craned back to the mirror. Paluzzi stood and sauntered to the window. He edged the drapes open and looked down to Cannon Street. It was getting darker and homebound evening traffic was trundling fast northwards. He wondered how long the street would remain closed on Friday. In a meditative tone he said, 'You'll have a good view of the President thing here.' The girl didn't reply. She had finished dressing and was zipping up. 'Do you have connections in the Isle of Man?' she said coolly. Paluzzi's face tautened. His eyes darted onto her. 'What are you talking about?' he snapped.

Serena plucked a letter and passport from the dresser and waved them in front of him. 'You're getting old,' she said. 'In Milan you were never so forgetful.' She handed the papers over. 'The letter's from the Isle of Man, gives a hotel address here and all. The passport's a fake. You left them behind on Sunday – in your topcoat. Dangerous.'

In a white fury Paluzzi took the papers, crossed to the electric fire and lit them. Serena watched him, saw the effort at control, the attempt to regulate breathing. Unprofessionalism more than anything irked him and it was a good feeling – a feeling of power – to be able to shake this man. But she knew the limits. Paluzzi was growing old, but he hadn't changed *that* much.

'You haven't learnt anything you're not supposed to know,' he said smoothly. He came over to her and placed his hands on her shoulders. The grip was powerful and she thought for a moment he was going to hurt her, punish her. 'I come here to you, Serena, because I trust you. You're a good girl. But you should have a better life. This club – ' He shrugged. 'It's not you. Some day soon you and me – we're gonna have a better life, eh?'

Caught in the web of his grip and his eyes and his voice, the girl nodded submissively. Paluzzi smiled. The doorbell shrilled. He moved to her dresser and said a quick word into the intercom. He came back to her with her cotton-print shawl between his fingers. With a girlish delicacy he fitted it about her neck. 'Now,' he smiled. 'Duty calls for both of us. Off you go to your roulette tables.'

'You've someone coming here?'

He escorted her politely to the door, talking soothingly. 'I'm meeting some old friends while I'm here – no more.'

In the doorway she turned to him. It was as well, she decided, to sort the facts out *now*. 'You're planning a job, aren't you?' she said. He sighed. 'It depends on my friends,' he said. 'Now – off you go.'

As Serena descended the stairs a tall man with piratical dark looks passed her, on the way up. He smiled nervously, keeping his head tilted forward and his eyes low. She didn't recognise him but guessed who he might be.

Paluzzi recognised him instantly. The men didn't greet each other formally and the dark-featured man came unspeakingly into the room and sat immediately, as if burdened by the news he carried.

Paluzzi stood over him calmly. 'Well?' he said.

The man said, 'My friends agree. It's on.'

'Good,' Paluzzi said, and he went to fetch a map of the city to plan the route for the 'hit'.

2

A stuttering farrago of noise from within and without the car kept Bonney awake. The awkward situation of Gifford's house at a T–junction forced him to park in the only reasonably covered area opposite – an alley framed by a disco, a button factory and a Wimpy Bar. His surveillance had commenced at eleven the previous night and the disco had raged till four. The dawn hours were punctuated by the accidental triggering of the factory's alarm system, the arrival of the early shift with their loud jokes and louder cranking of machines, then the coming of the first trading vans. Twice Bonney had been obliged to move his car and twice he had been approached by hookers. For a brief spell, from seven or so, respite came. The thunder of the factory machines became a distant sleepy ululation, traffic sounds diminished and the stiffness of his muscles gave way to languorous ease. Nothing stirred at Gifford's house and he might almost have conceded to sleep had it not been for the irregular cackle of the UHF transceiver. The vigil had seemed a waste of time till nine o'clock. Bonney had been about to radio for relief when, at last, Gifford showed. He had radioed base instead and instructed them to contact Hackett. The return message had said Hackett would be on the spot in twenty minutes. Now, after less than fifteen, a Panda cruised past the corner and dropped him off.

He flopped into the car beside Bonney. 'By himself?'

'Yeah. Looked sober enough. Doubt if he was on a bender.'

Hackett nodded. *He* looked pretty rough, Bonny observed. His hair was tousled and wet from a shower and his eyes looked glazed and sunken. Bonney knew he had had his first kip in forty-eight hours that night and suspected he had already been up and about for an hour or more.

'Nothing at all happened since eleven?'

'My virginity was threatened.'

'I mean, with Rip van Winkle.'

'Nope. That's his first show. Are you going straight in?'

'Nothing like the present.' Hackett pulled the door of the car open. As if responding to cue, the front door of the house under observation reopened and a short man in a grey mac tottered out.

'By Christ, he's back.' Disappointment coloured Bonney's voice. He had hoped for quick action and a return to home and bed. Now, if Gifford kept moving, it would mean a follow. And experience had taught Bonney that the only short follows were the ones you effected with a warrant in your hands.

'Tail 'im,' Hackett said.

They sat for a moment, watching the shuffling figure move away from them, headed off down the side street. Then the man turned quickly right and vanished. Bonney fired the engine and the car pulled slowly off. The UHF squawked out briefly, asking if Hackett would be attending Havelock's planning meeting at ten. Hackett said no, that he had arranged talks with Pemberton and a FBI man and would see Detective Chief Super Havelock later in the day. He signed off.

'That's the problem with a caper like this,' he said absently. 'Every move of every man pre-planned. Every conceivable contingency accounted for on paper. And while that's going on we're out of action, off the streets giving Dick Turpin time to think of the contingency we didn't think of. Like bloody chess. You've got to keep thinking but you've got to keep moving too.'

They swerved into a cul-de-sac turn-off in time to see Gifford climb into a rust-bitten Morris van.

'Past him, past him,' Hackett hissed. Bonney accelerated, moved fast down the street and swung in between two parked vans. He rolled down the street and swung in between two parked vans. He rolled down his window and adjusted his clip-mirror. 'He's going. For the centre.'

'Follow.'

Bonney pulled into a wide U and sped off after the Morris. Momentarily they lost him at the T-junction but, assuming the city centre route rather than the docks, they headed north and picked him up again in the stodgy flow of breakfast traffic.

Bonney refrained from attempting conversation with his boss. In two years he had come to accept, if not understand, the almost prismatic graduations of Hackett's character. His moods, he saw, were dictated solely by the fears and failures – and successes – of the job. And he had a chameleon capacity for change. Dour and brooding for days, the smallest of victories won by the most junior of his men could change him totally and the rise to near euphoria would be selfless and communicated to everyone. In his philosophical moments Bonney was reminded of sanguine heroes of fiction who lived for dare-devilry and whose lives were measured in villains killed. The comparison made him laugh, but that didn't disparage the reality of it. Hackett was, as so many had told him from his first day on the Squad, a dangerous and dirty bastard. But, in a dangerous and dirty job, he was the best kind of bastard – an ambitious and dedicated pro who intended to outrun the opposition not only to enhance his position but to make sure he stayed alive. Bonney liked working with him just as he liked riding the fastest motor bikes and entertaining intelligent women: very little was for show and the priorities were right.

Now, after last night's base conference on targets running, Bonney suspected the cause of Hackett's morose silence. When Hackett didn't open up he said at last, 'Any news on Paluzzi?'

The answer came pat. Hackett had been thinking of Paluzzi. 'Got together a fair picture of his movements from Interpol and the American Narcotics Bureau. He's been in retirement. Had a share in a cover factory relaying watered-down dope to Austria, Germany. The Narcotics Bureau were after it for years. Finally put in a plant, as far as I could make out, and closed the place down. Manager got ten years. There were four or five Italian-resident directors. They all got various slaps on the knuckles. The Bureau wanted Paluzzi but someone pulled him out fast. He stayed clean. He's been living in Berne, visiting Paris, keeping low. No convictions since he's been last here. Not surprising.'

'You really expected him to set up again? Where? – London?'

'God knows. He avoided London last time – stuck to here. London's sealed up, too many little Hitlers. All that's left there is porno, protection for ex-pros and Soho. Not Paluzzi's style.'

Gifford's Morris braked for traffic lights and Bonney rolled up behind him. Bonney had been hesitant about getting close and being 'clocked', but Hackett was in reckless form. 'I haven't got all day to tour the bloody city. Want to talk to him anyway.'

'Will I pull him in?'

'Give him five minutes.'

The old Morris staggered back into life but veered off westwards, away from the city. The unmarked squad car followed.

'I think he knows we're following. He's hotting up.' Bonney crashed back a gear and overtook a dawdling lorry. The Morris had led them to a built-up, labyrinthine part of the city – through an area of new housing estates and sprawling factory complexes. Ahead now, as they turned on to a two-mile-long broad straight road, the little car rushed up to full speed, weaving adroitly in and out of the crooked traffic line.

'The church!' Hacket barked. 'Watch the bloody church. He might try to dip there.'

A mile up, the spiral of a massive church shadowed the road. Bonney could see clustered knots of people moving round the entrance gates and a procession of cars edging in and out of a marked parking area within the grounds. It was a wedding or a funeral – an ideal jump-off location for a pursued car. 'Get up – faster!' Hackett said. As he spoke, the traffic was thickening round them. A tail-back caused by the egress of cars from the church brought them to a dead stop and they lost sight of the Morris. There was a moment of suspension – Hackett and Bonney sat motionless, staring ahead, eyes dilated, brains charging. Bonney was fractionally faster at reaching a decision. He edged forward, cutting into on-coming traffic, headlights blazing. An inevitable storm of protest reared up. Klaxons roared and a double-decker bus swerved sharply to avoid hitting the squad car broadside-on. The driver whipped back his window to curse them in a stentorian rage. Bonney pushed forward and drew level with the church gates just as the main stream of traffic started to roll again. Hackett jumped out of the car, glanced across the moving traffic.

'Can't see him,' he shouted. Bonney left the engine running and clambered out. He looked up and down the road. Plenty of traffic, no Gifford. He looked over to the growing group on the church steps. The car park, he saw, was almost full. Thirty, forty cars their roofs sparkling white in the sun like an undulating pool. Impossible to distinguish one grey Morris from the pack. Hackett called over to him. 'Got your Cub?'

Bonney understood. He leant back into the car and pulled out his Ultra Cub radio. A small VHF piece, its range of two or three hundred yards would enable them to split the search. 'Don't want to lose him, 'case he thinks we're after him,' Hackett shouted. 'You try the grounds. I'll follow the traffic. Wait for me.'

As Bonney skipped through the thread of cars, Hackett took the wheel and started bending the rules. He motored as far as he could on the right-hand side of the road, eyeing the on-going cars carefully as he advanced, then cut diagonally through the stream and mounted the wide footpath. He drove no more than a half-mile when he caught sight of the Morris again. 'Poor Bonney,' he grinned to himself, then elbowed back into the road traffic.

The follow didn't last much longer. At the top of the church road the Morris pointed citywards again, covered another mile then stopped at a pub in a narrow shopping street. Hackett pulled in a hundred yards back and watched. The small man knocked repeatedly on the pub door but no one answered. With a disgruntled shrug he moved on down the street and entered a café. Hackett got out of the car and ambled down to see what was happening. He had hoped Gifford might be heading for a meet, but it seemed unlikely somehow. Certainly, Hackett felt, the man hadn't guessed he was being tailed. There had been no open attempt to shake the squad car off and nothing unusual about the route. Gifford had merely taken a circular track to avoid city congestion and driven from south to north of the built-up central area. Now, as Hackett watched him from the news vendor's stall across the street, nothing in the man's posture or expression reflected anything other than dejection and tiredness. Hackett stalled while Gifford drank down a cup of brew, ate a sandwich and surveyed the passers-by with vague eyes. Then he left the café and crossed to a betting shop. Hackett followed, morning paper in hand.

Inside, the wide arena was inhabited by only a half-dozen customers studying the morning news sheets for the early races. Hackett drifted casually in, his own paper opened to the racing page, his eyes tripping indifferently to the faces round the wall. He recognised none.

Gifford was standing at yesterday's board, studying the Liverpool card. The greyness of his clothes seemed to suffuse his face and he looked quite different from the face on the D/F. Less alive, for one thing, Hackett mused. He moved up to Liverpool. Gifford didn't look down. Gifford prodded a finger at the winner of the 2.45 and cursed.

'Miss a winner?' Hackett said evenly.

'That's the bitch of it! I never fail, get 'em all, but what bloody good does it do me with not a spick down.' He jabbed the finger out again. 'That son-of-a-bugger was bound to hit home with the going soft – weren't it?'

'No job, then?'

The little man froze and Hackett heard him swallow. He moved off. Hackett strolled after him. They were positioned in a corner now, far from the nearest punter and well out of earshot. Hackett knew he'd broken through to the man; the tone of his voice had carried sarcasm and double-meaning. Now, Hackett guessed, Gifford would be trying to decide whether Hackett was cop or convict. 'Left Hammersmith, have you?'

The eyes still didn't turn to him. 'Why?'

'On the game?'

'Bugger off, you stupid bastard.' Gifford went to walk away. Hackett took his arm firmly.

'Hey now – no offence meant. You should be glad of your fame. I mean, you're a star trouper. I recognised the face.'

Slowly, like a mischievous schoolboy, Gifford stared up

to Hackett. 'What you want – me bleeding autograph?'

Hackett winked, held a smile. 'What brings you here? Remember the old rules. Territory and all that.' The smile widened to menace. 'Well, you're in mine – right?'

'Meaning – Crime Squad?'

'They teach you something at Leicester.'

'I don't want no bleeding trouble, mate. I'm here 'cause I was offered a job here – a legit job.'

'Where?'

'Fell through. Not nice. But that's life. You can't trust no one no more.'

'So why are you staying here?'

'See the President on Friday.'

'Who's keeping you company?'

'I'm fifty, mate. Don't need company 'less I'm celebrating and I don't often do that.'

'Like to do me a favour?'

A petulant flush heightened Gifford's colour, making him look almost human. But there was no indignation in the voice. 'Who are you trying to bloody crucify now?'

'No one. Just asking round. Finding out. What could you tell me for fifty quid?'

'I'm not well connected here. You know that, I'm sure. South London's my beat. Or don't the Flying Squad file reports anymore?'

'Sure. But you're in a league of your own. Big name.' Hackett spoke flatly and Gifford wasn't sure of his meaning. The smile on the young bloke's face had faded and he looked a reasonable sort, despite the Squad tag. Gifford was always receptive to 'reasonable' propositions. He said so, in a roundabout way. Hackett said, 'An old friend of yours – Frank Paluzzi – is around. . . .' He expected he'd have to push that, but Gifford took it coolly. 'I know,' he said. 'No one's counting him for dead yet.'

'Where is he?'

Gifford laughed, chortling from the mouth as if doing an awkward trick from memory. 'Jesus, if I had tabs on Paluzzi I'd sell to the highest bidder. You could put your fifty up your snort.'

'Know what he's up to?'

'No.'

'A hit?'

'Dunno. Some say. Others don't. He's not got many mates hereabouts.'

'But he's got you.' Hackett frowned. 'You said 'here-abouts'. Is he planning visiting us again? I thought we put the breeze in him five years back.' Christ, Hackett was thinking, could I be that lucky?

'I've heard talk,' Gifford said, then he shut up quickly and diverted his attention back to the board.

'Has he been in touch with you?' Hackett pursued.

Gifford shook his head and directed a vulpine glance to Hackett. 'I'll see what I can get you – for a hundred.'

'Fifty.'

'Seventy-five.'

'Fifty.'

He shrugged, pulled Hackett's paper off him and stuffed it into his mac. 'You think he's going to try the Yankie boy, don't you? Wouldn't put it past 'im – eh? Good contract from the Ruskies?' He giggled. 'Or the Maff?' He turned to go and Hackett motioned to intercept him, check him. Gifford smiled gaily. 'Don't fret, kiddo. See you at Vino's – the café opposite. Give me till seven. And have the cash – OK?'

Hackett watched the man waddle off and was reminded of the docile, aged pigeons that haunted the courtyard park at headquarters, tragic and tame, like fallen angels. He was well familiar with the post-prison symptoms of lethargy and passiveness which affected a certain breed of criminal and guessed that Gifford had been one of the type that bent with the strain. He wondered what sort of man he was all those years ago, but he sensed that ten years of the institutional cossetting of Parkhurst and Leicester had changed him considerably and that his participation in a major crime was unlikely.

A subdued excitement perked him as he trotted back to his car. A link in the chain to Paluzzi had been forged. He was getting nearer. And this time, for Paluzzi, there would be no getaway.

Hackett's mood had changed from black to grey.

The bad news came through at three-fifteen.

Hackett had driven to the airport to collect Louise and her male companion from the Squad whose pursuit of the immigrant organiser had fouled up again in Paris. The UHF called him in, instructing that vital news had come through. He reached headquarters in a half-hour and was called into the Intelligence Bureau on the second floor where Tate was carrying out an impromptu evaluation meeting with a few Squad and Branch men. Havelock looked in briefly, said he had to drive north to meet the American Embassy's Legal Attaché and departed. The telex was rattling away and the UHF in the inner room seemed unnaturally lively. Before anyone specified the cause of upheaval, Hackett knew it concerned the major operation running, the Presidential visit. There were too many strained faces, too much crosstalk for it to be in connection with a standard target run. Tate came across to him.

'Pemberton's boys picked up a bit of dirty talk. Sound source, they say. On our payroll. Says someone's looking for a Shot for Friday.'

Hackett said nothing. The implication of Tate's news stunned him. Threats on the lives of public figures – whether from anonymous crack-pot or militant faction –

were staple fare, almost an accepted part of the game when travel and personal appearances were scheduled, but Intelligence information like this was as good – or as bad – as a primed gun on the day. Pemberton wasn't an alarmist, Hackett knew. His underworld links were solid and his *modus operandi* admirable. If he set down there was an assassination job being planned then it became a hard issue of trying to weed out an assassin, his method and his motive.

'We're going to have to go after this one,' Tate said tensely. 'Pemberton is on to his lead now, trying to dig up names, but he's not hopeful. The President himself will be consulted and Havelock is giving a full account to the FBI at the Embassy. But it'll go ahead. No doubt about that. We'll just have to tighten up so as nobody gets the chance to pull a trigger.'

'Virtually impossible,' Hackett mumbled, thinking aloud. Tate grunted in annoyance. 'We'll have to make it possible, won't we? What about your friends? Any action at all? Anything risky?'

'Saw Gifford. He seems clean. But Paluzzi could be in business.'

'If it's him, I want him before Friday. His track record for getting away is too good.'

'I'm following it up. For fifty pounds from the Imprest fund Gifford's promising me stories.'

A winy whiff of after-shave heralded Burgess who sidled up with pallor suffusing his sour expression. Hackett asked if there was anything on Paluzzi and he said no. In an uncommonly civil tone he asked Hackett what prospects the squad and branch had for chasing a gunman down at such short notice.

'Good, if we get the breaks,' Hackett said. 'But a lot depends on the people we're up against.' He frowned thoughtfully for a second. 'That's worth considering, you know,' he went on. 'Who exactly are we likely to be pitching against? If it's a large organisation – say the Mafia – they'd import a shot, avoid this kind of possible leak.'

Tate cut in. 'No one's averse to using good cut-outs, middle men.'

'But it's unlikely that a committed organisation would leave it as late as this to scour around.'

Burgess' starched look softened and surprise widened his eyes. Mentally, ruefully, Hackett noted it. Burgess' theory of class division within the force accounted for gods and gladiators, with nothing in between; the gods, like himself, did the thinking; the lesser mortals enforced law on the streets. People like Hackett didn't exist – or shouldn't.

'There's a marked chance it's all a diversion,' Hackett continued. 'Sensible. As it is we'll be stretched on Friday. Every man we have will be out there, backing up the President business. Now, with this fire-cracker, we'll be stretched further.'

'Diversion to what?' Tate saw Hackett's reasoning. But the argument would lead them into hypotheses when, with time so much against them, they desperately needed to stick to facts.

'Anything,' Hackett enthused. 'Dope. There's the two-day pop festival in Sladevale starting tomorrow. That'll attract thousands. There's God-knows-how-much moving in wages and security items – the standard Friday traffic, last week of the month. There's junk from ancient Greece going up to the British Museum – worth a couple of bob, without doubt. I think there's a bullion train. Force Operations Room will have all the movements. Any one of them could be the real aim. The state visit limits *our* movements and makes the perfect diversion.'

'We'd never cover them all,' Tate said blankly, the weight of Hackett's argument seeping in.

'And anyway it'd be too risky to try,' Hackett admitted

frankly. 'On Friday, if we're still guessing in the dark, our safest course is to give all we can to cover on the procession route – but we've got more than thirty-six working hours till then. What we need to do is look to the kind of people who'd be clever enough to set up this sort of deception and who might be trying something big. Immediately our field is limited. No doubt we're talking about professionals . . .'

'The likes of Paluzzi,' Tate said wryly.

'There may be more,' Hackett expanded. 'I think we need to get together – all the boys – and examine our running targets.'

'You got Gifford's info, I take it?' Burgess said.

'Yes. It's been helpful. We might get through to Paluzzi there. I've spoken to Gifford.'

'You have him under surveillance?'

'Not now, no.'

'Burgess clicked his tongue in admonition. 'I should imagine that would be top consideration. A psychopathic bloody lunatic with kidnapping and menace charges behind him! I'd have trumped something up, pulled him in as soon as I knew he was here, if only for the duration of the visit.'

It was too easy to smart under Burgess' outbursts, but counter-attacking was never worth the energy expended. Hackett had long since copped this and had come to treat the squalls in Burgess' manner as meaningless aberrations. But direct criticism of his methods from any quarter piqued Hackett more than a little. 'Look,' he said heatedly, 'we have a situation where every man and woman on the force in this town is over-burdened. My squad people are no exception – principal responsibility falls to us to try to predetermine what's going to happen. I know the rules, I know how the customers operate. I've seen enough Giffords in my time to know how far I can push 'em and how far I can trust 'em.' Recoiling from Hackett's shout, Burgess' blanched expression returned. 'Number one,' Hackett went on, 'a sure way of losing a grasser you have in your pocket is to doubt him and follow. And number two – even if I did suspect Gifford might be into a job here I'd be hard pressed to free a man to set up a tail. We've too much else going – and there's just nothing to suggest Gifford is at it. He's been out for two years and he's stayed as clean as a whistle. That's all I've got to go by – and my own bloody judgement. And my judgement says Gifford is out of the game!'

'A couple of years downstairs doesn't change every criminal,' Burgess offered defensively.

'But it changes some. Gifford could be one. He's fifty, maybe he's past sprinting down streets and jumping over walls.'

'Abney's damn' near fifty too, but it hasn't hampered him.' Burgess saw Hackett's face tighten. 'All those boys – the Big Five involved in the kidnapping – they all had long tough careers behind them. I got the D/Fs you were looking for with some notes from the CRO people. They make heavy reading. Three of 'em – King, Robertson and Gifford – were involved in military operations in Africa at various stages. The other two, Abney and Pridell, have lively East End pedigrees – associated with teams like the Krays.'

'Are any of them at it just now?' Hackett snapped. 'Where did you leave the info?'

'On your desk.' Burgess' tone had modulated to eager helpfulness. 'They'd been keeping an eye on Abney in the Met. Suspicion of living off immoral earnings. Bit of a lecher, from what I could see. Only interest outside crime is women.'

'How 'bout the others?'

Burgess shrugged. 'Look OK, but what else would you expect? Robertson and Pridell are just off parole. But I wouldn't trust one of the bunch.'

'I take it they all hang around the Met?'

'So it seems.'

A pretty clerk interrupted to say Burgess was wanted on the telephone. Burgess excused himself and moved off. Tate had been busying himself lighting a pipe. He had refrained from the talk but had listened to every word. Now he said, 'The Big Five's worth looking at, if only to place their present movements and count them out.'

Hackett nodded. 'I'll play Gifford my own way, but I'll put someone on to checking the others down. If there's anything promising on the CROs I'll look into it myself.' Leaving Tate to resume his briefing, Hackett headed for the canteen where he located a follow team of two girls and a man who had just commenced duty after an all-night shift. Together they returned to his office where he checked the D/Fs and CRO notes and gave them a quick discourse on the new threat of the Presidential visit. He then detailed them to the task of searching down the Big Five with whatever help the Yard and C-11 could provide. Precise accounts of their existences since prison were required, he ordered. The team head left and Hackett was making tracks for the canteen to catch up with his own lunch when the tannoy blared his name and he was derouted to Force Operations Room.

There, with Havelock (breathlessly back from a ten minute meeting), Pemberton and a FBI man, a discussion into outpacing the enemy began.

The FBI man made it clear that the President would not call off his trip. The assassination bid would have to be foiled in the field.

A damp March drizzle that clouded the streets like sea fog brought premature night to the city.

Hackett reached Vino's Café early and took advantage of

the arranged meet location to enjoy his first meal of the day. The rock salmon was rock tough and the bosomy waitress with winking holes in her tights became tiresome after a while with her leery smiles and curious, loaded stares. But it was good to be able to sit, rest and eat. Hackett ignored the pushy girl, burrowed himself in a patron's abandoned magazine and kept an eye on his watch. At seven there was no sign of Gifford and by a quarter past indefinable intuition told him something was wrong.

He changed his seat to a bench near the window, sipped tea and surveyed the busy street. Bonney, he knew, was cruising casually, keeping the café under loose watch, but there was no sign of him now. The fifty quid in fives was in his pocket and, as he thought about Gifford, it came forcibly home to him that it would take a lot to make that kind of tramp turn down a chance to collect having agreed to the principle of cash and info. With the reflex action of the man who has been through this particular ritual scores of times, Hackett quickly re-enacted this morning's conversation with Gifford in his mind. The idea of giving information hadn't been repugnant to the man and he had seemed easy-going about grassing, particularly, on Paluzzi. The fifty quid was debated, but that had been settled on. The man had no fears, no reservations, as far as Hackett could see. He had been willing. And now – with half-seven ringing on the ornate wall clock – he hadn't followed through. Why? What had put him off? The obvious couldn't be excluded – that he had failed to get the info, or had been warned off – but Hackett knew this breed of fish, the grasser, better than most. Once they got the flavour of the bait, once they were hungry enough, they rarely let go.

At eight, seeing Bonney roll by, Hackett left the café and rejoined him. He explained the position and told Bonney to drive back to Gifford's digs.

The caretaker in the near-derelict Victorian house

allowed them in unquestioningly but told them he believed Mr Chadley – ('That's the man what drives the Morris') – had left. It didn't trouble him because he knew Mr Chadley had paid the landlord one week in advance.

The room Hackett and Bonney were led to was dank, near-empty and smelt of desertion. Having shaken off the caretaker (from whom they learnt that the client had no friends in and took no phone calls), Bonney and Hackett began systematically going over the room, checking drawers, wardrobes and bedclothes. They found nothing, not as much as a broken comb. Gifford had, for reasons unknown, packed carefully and made a clean departure.

Dismayed, they sought out the caretaker again and questioned him further. Had Gifford spoken to him? Never. Had he claimed to be working, or perhaps on holiday? He never said. How long had he planned staying? One week was paid for – God knows after that. When did the caretaker last see him? The man scratched his head, sucked on his briar pipe. ''Bout five, I'd say. Came in, very busy, very red in the face. Rushed on up. I heard him moving round, heard doors banging. Guessed he might be shiftin'.'

With words of thanks, Hackett and Bonney resumed the street. The mist was backing off and the rain had died. The roads looked oiled and bright and the scent of early wallflowers rode on the night wind. Bonney said, 'Maybe he was bluffing you, about the info.'

Hackett shook his head. Gifford had meant what he said, had intended to grass, to give what he could. 'Looks to me like someone scared him off,' he said, but with little conviction in the words. They climbed back into the car and sat in silence for several minutes. Then Hackett said, 'It's not right. My instinct tells me. Something big, something really big pulled Gifford away.' He smiled lamely to Bonney. 'You've a long drive ahead of you, old son. Back to base first – I want to see what Cook has brought me in on the Big Five. Then we'll try Hammersmith. Gifford's mother.'

In a muffled tone, addressing the steering wheel, Bonney cursed someone as the son of a whore. It might have meant Gifford, but he was thinking more specifically of Hackett. With twelve hours leave in two days, it was his turn for sleepless living.

At headquarters Hackett found Woman Detective Sergeant Jennie Cook, senior of the team assigned to the Big Five job, and was promptly presented with an enormous 'coincidence' tale. The Yard had been most co-operative and the CRO had lent every assistance. Each of the Five had been traced to family addresses and three had current job addresses. None had been in trouble since their release but one of the team, Stanley Abney, had been under surveillance from CID, suspected of pimping. But, for the best part, that was the end of the line. Cook's attempts to establish individual whereabouts fell flat. Only Abney and Gifford were traceable – Abney at a South London address and Gifford via local CID info. The other three had vanished. According to family information, King and Pridell had gone on holidays – where exactly, no one was quite sure; and Robertson's mother claimed her son had been 'called away on offer of work, to Manchester.'

These compiled details, neatly typed in a folder in Hackett's hands, demanded fuller investigation and Cook had neatly post-scripted her initial report with the note: 'Further inquiries now being made at King's, Pridell's and Abney's job addresses.'

'This stinks to high heaven,' Hackett remarked. 'Have you got anywhere with the jobs?'

Jennie Cook, a recent recruit to the Squad, had learnt quickly to translate and manage Hackett's moods. She shrugged her masculine shoulders, gesturing helplessness. 'Most of what's there we only got in the last two hours. It doesn't look like we'll get far with the jobs tonight.'

'Abney – did you bother to check him?'

'Yes. No answer at the flat, but tomorrow we could try . . .'

"Ten of Hearts' – what's this? A club? Shop?'

'According to CRO it's a . . . well, sauna club . . . something like that.'

Hackett's breath sang through his teeth. He shot a baleful look at Jennie Cook. 'Christ! You don't think that'll be a nine-to-five branch of the Civil Service, do you? Massage parlour. Stock stuff – a prefab sauna room, two plastic shower units, three big-titted girls, a manageress who can't speak English and an eternal supply of Vaseline.'

Jennie held Hackett's defiant stare and Bonney choked a cough to cover mounting laughter. 'I'm sorry,' she said, 'we didn't cop that. Otherwise I'd have followed it up immediately. I'd intended checking in the morning.'

'We don't *have* till the morning!' Hackett barked. 'Tomorrow's too bloody late if something is brewing. We need every second we can get!' His voice cut out quickly but the clear ring of what he had said rebounded in the little room. Jennie stood up and pulled the canvas hood over her typewriter. Bonney could see the tremulous movements of her lips and the hesitancy of her actions; he knew she was upset.

It wasn't that Hackett had insulted feminine sensibilities, but she had been stalling, working to her own pace, and now – suddenly – she was realising the veracity of his comments. 'I'll drive on up to London myself,' she said, pulling on her coat. Her words were flat, matter-of-fact, not self-pitying.

From the filing cabinets across the room Hackett swivelled and smiled stiffly over to her. 'No, love. We'll take it. I want to get to Gifford – so we'll want to drive up anyway.' He walked to her, looped his arms round her waist. Boldly she faced him, a flicker of injured professional pride weakening her gaze. 'You've been good,' he said softly. 'Ninety per cent. It's just that tonight, tomorrow, we need a hundred or nothing.' She nodded. In a gentle, friendly way, he broke his grip round her waist and slapped her on the bottom.

'Discrimination,' Bonney quipped. 'He never does that to male officers.'

Hackett took him in a swift, painless head-lock. 'Right, Blue Eyes,' he chimed. 'Let's you and me go for a drive in the country and we'll make amends.'

Jennie Cook laughed and turned to the phone on her desk which had begun to ring with the special urgency of night-time phones.

The girl with the short bubbly curtains of blonde hair smiled with a kind of well-worn charm as Hackett approached the reception desk. There was a second of silent mutual consideration and the electrical signals richochetted back and forth. Each found the other sexually attractive and, as Hackett glanced around, he decided this was just the kind of place, of ambience, where such an attraction might be profitably explored. The outside of the building was plain and businesslike, with just a brass plaque to announce the nature of the service, but inside, with rich-coloured carpets, exotic wall tapestries, soft light, silk and warmth, the uncertain spirit was quenched and subjugated in a flash by the violet eyes of the blonde mistress of the manor.

'Have you an appointment, sir?' The accent was distinguishably Cockney, but slower, tamed.

'No, I'm a friend of Mr – er – Abney's. The boss.'

Hackett had been unwilling to possibly scare Abney with the formal approach.

'He's not the boss,' the girl said politely. Her eyes tripped over Hackett again, not in admiration now but in blunt inspection. 'What is it for?'

'I know him – from old times.'

The large full lips stretched downwards, acknowledging and – maybe – approving. 'I see. Well, I hope you haven't come far 'cause he's not around. I don't know where he is.'

'I tried his flat . . . .'

'Not *his* flat,' the girl rasped. 'Mine.' A small frown ruckled her pretty brow. Hackett got the score. Abney had always been a womaniser, a free-wheeler who preferred the easy control of women to the democratic strife of a close-knit male team. From his criminal history, Hackett had seen, the Big Five kidnap job had been a non-typical working arrangement. This lush haven would be more Abney's style.

'Do you expect him back soon?' Hackett urged.

'Never, for all I care.' The speed and zest of the statement hinted at a lovers' quarrel. Hackett carefully said so, at which juncture the girl stood up and smiled grimly. Another staff girl had materialised and the blonde receptionist asked her to take over. She turned to Hackett. 'Come on,' she said, tossing her head towards a door at the back of the room. 'Have a drink with me and tell me about Stan.'

Following her, Hackett went through to a small grey-and-red room that doubled for bar and cloakroom. Manet prints of nudes in gilt frames lined the walls. Amid the skeins of unclad limbs, clothes – even the gear that hung about on the wall racks – seemed somehow unsuitable in this luxury room. Hackett found himself eyeing the plump rounds of the blonde, picturing her among the Manets. The girl went behind the teak-frame bar and began pouring drinks. Hackett declined alcohol, settled for a mineral. She poured herself a whiskey, sat across the bar-top and stared deeply into his eyes. 'You're a copper, aren't you?' she said quietly.

There was no point denying it. Hackett said he was, but repeated that he needed to speak to Abney – on an urgent matter not connected with his record.

'We get so many coppers round here you learn to tell them by their doggie manner. Harmless types. Never know where to put their eyes.'

'None of my friends call me harmless,' Hackett said. 'And I always know where to put . . . everything.' The girl threw her head back and laughed explosively. 'Cheeky fella,' she said. 'Makes a welcome change.' Her expression grew quickly serious. 'Then you're not trying to make out we're still running tarts here?'

'I'm not interested in that. I'd never be so insensitive as to accuse someone as, well, cute as you of anything like that. That's right outside your class.' The lie echoed thinly; Hackett remembered where he had used the 'confidence' approach before – with Gifford. Its success then had been limited. But the blonde took it well. A veteran of con men, Hackett mused.

'For what it's worth, you'd be dead right. I'm not into that end of things. I'm a chiropodist. Certificates and all that. And this place is legit – most of the time. We have a good trade from the hotels up the road. The brass plaque puts the hookers off and the dirty old men stick to the West End for their hand-jobs. So it's nice here.'

'And where does Stan Abney come in? He works here?'

The girl pulled a face. 'The bum. Work? Not our Stan. Sure, he worked for a while as a handyman. Painted ceilings. I fixed it up for him eighteen months ago, to keep the parole people happy.'

'Who owns the place?'

'German husband and wife. Real krauts. Waffen-SS and all that. We don't see much of them, but they'll be registered with the Yard by now if you want to check up. A woman called Julie Johns runs the place.'

'So where's Stan?' Hackett smiled.

The girl took a long draught at her whiskey, closed her eyes tight. 'Don't know. Can't even guess. The bastard lives with me, at my flat in Putney. But that's gonna stop as from tonight.' She sighed plaintively. 'He's an unreliable swine. Two days ago I woke up and found a note. 'Gone away for a couple of days.' Full stop. Probably met some chick . . .' The girl's voice wavered and she put her mouth back to her drink.

'Does he often skip like that?'

She shook her head. 'Not really. He likes to keep in my circle 'cause of the girls, I think. He's a girls' man.' Her eyes fixed back on Hackett's. 'Is that why you want him – something to do with tarts?'

'No.' Hackett believed in the sincerity of the girl, guessed that her role with Abney – as any woman's role would be – was passionate but remote. He said, 'Did you ever hear of Frank Paluzzi, a friend of Stan's?'

The violet eyes narrowed, thinking. 'One of the fellas he went to jail with?' She shook her golden locks. 'I know Stan avoided most of his old cronies. Said they brought back unhappy memories. The failure of that . . . business really cut him up. Even more than the sentence inside.'

'Likes to win, does he?'

'All the time. That's Stan. Money and women and winning all the time – that's his life. That last job really cut him up, made him very bitter.'

For ten more minutes Hackett chatted, cajoling and questioning, and it became clearly apparent that the girl was aware of most of Abney's movements since prison, was aware that he collected small cash by pimping two prostitutes and that he still had friends on the fringe of big London crime; but it became equally clear that, to the best of her knowledge, no link remained between Abney and the Big Five team. He asked a few questions about the associates the girl knew then said, 'One way or the other I've got to get in touch with him. It's important. So I'll ask you to do me a favour.'

The generous bust heaved and the cat-eyes opened wide. She moved slightly closer, smiling a little, and Hackett caught the insidious scent of her body. 'Anything at all you want,' she said warmly.

He diverted his thoughts. 'If anything comes up – if you remember anyone you think Stan might have gone to – or if he gets in touch . . .?'

'I'll give you a call.' She thought twice. 'I hope he's not . . . I hope you don't think he's at it again?'

'I doubt it. But for his own good – and mine – get in touch if you hear anything, or remember anything.' Hackett jotted down the squad number and his own extension. She saw the regional code and drew a sharp breath. 'Wow – all this way to see old Stan! Must be important to one of you.'

He stood to leave and the girl came out from behind the bar. 'By the way,' she said, producing a business-card from the pocket of her smock, 'my name is Dink. Short for Diana and a thousand other things.'

'I'll remember where to come if I want to be chir-opped,' Hackett grinned. He patted her arm and left. Walking back to the car, the confident feeling of having made a good ally in the opposition camp cheered him but the ominous face of the electronic clock over the bank opposite interposed the facts and the hopes. It was nearing midnight. Paluzzi was somewhere in Britain and the Big Five, his alleged strike-team for one notorious hit, had disappeared. Tomorrow the American President would arrive and in thirty-six hours he'd be flying south. And someone, somewhere was threatening to kill him. Hackett was resolved to make sure the hit didn't happen, but even more than that he wanted Paluzzi. There was no definite indication of connection between Paluzzi and the presidential threat but Hackett *wanted* one, wanted Paluzzi to stick his neck out. This warped aspect of his reasoning didn't bother him. Only one thought dominated his mind – getting back at Paluzzi, making up for five years ago. Intermittent images, like moving film through a broken projector, flickered through his mind: Paluzzi's arms boat, the stake-out, the squad's counter set-up, the preparations for ambush, the first shots fired, the endless fight at the docks . . . .

Like all the jobs he'd been on – good and bad – in revived memory the details irritated him. He made mistakes. He shouldn't have made mistakes. Paluzzi should never have got away.

In the shadows of the car Bonney was seated bolt-upright, restless behind the wheel. Hackett told him they were out of luck, that Abney was gone.

'I tuned into the Yard frequency. They gave me a bit of news. The game's well in play. Anonymous phone call came over a half-hour ago, threatening the President's life.'

Hackett swallowed the word indifferently. He consulted a note from CRO he had extracted from Jennie Cook's file. 'Right,' he sighed. 'Whether it is a diversion or not we're a hundred miles here from the scene of the action, so we'd best get back. Tomorrow'll be taken up with route planning and distribution of manpower so we're up against it.' He dropped the file. 'What have we got? Full checks – car, house, flat on Gifford, ditto similar on Abney – and we get nothing. And according to this . . .' He tapped the file notes.

'You reckon the old kidnap team have rebanded?' Bonney's clipped tone made it a rhetorical question.

Hackett shrugged. 'Drive to the Yard first. Want to have

a word with someone in C-12 or the Flying Squad, might give some lead on Abney.'

Bonney put the car in gear. It was midnight.

3

When Stanley Abney rose on Thursday morning at eleven and pulled back the curtains he saw the crisp bleak cover of the first snow of spring draped over everything. His first reaction was to stand and gaze in awe-struck admiration at the pristine glory of the scene, then his heart leapt in his chest and he remembered that bad weather meant trouble. Snow in particular might jeopardise the entire operation. Pulling his trousers quickly on, he ran downstairs in search of Pridell and King.

He found Pridell in the kitchen reading the morning newspaper and lazily chewing toast. Nothing in the huge man's pose suggested fluster or unease.

'The bloody snow!' Abney shouted.

Pridell's piggy eyes shot up at him. 'It's okay. Slight cover. Barometer's rapidly on the way up. Doubt if it'll be a problem.'

'By Jesus, it better not be.' Abney stormed acrosss to the window and looked out. The professional calm of Pridell and the others always bothered him. With the exception of Gifford whose day, he reckoned, had gone, the team were heartless, inhuman savages whom it was never wise to trust too long. And yet he had trusted them before, and served a long stretch for his labours and loyalty – and he would do it again. The fascination, he had long since decided, was their fearlessness and their style. Before the fouled kidnap job they had had four or five good years together. They had always thought big, and had pulled a couple of large-scale jobs and got away stock free. And they still had the capacity for big hits. Abney was certain of that. *He* had the talent and the team had the talent. He was prepared to gamble for £20,000 plus on that.

The countryside sparkled in jewelled light as the sun broke the clouds and, as Abney watched, a green Jaguar car curled off the main road a mile away and angled up the winding lane that led to the farmhouse. King's voice bloomed up behind him. 'We're on. Here's Robertson with Giff.' Abney nodded and King joined him at the window, the binoculars through which he had identified the occupants of the car strung round his neck. 'Thought Giff mightn't come,' King said. 'Must need the cash badly.'

Parking the Jag in an outhouse, Robertson and Gifford entered the farmhouse via the backdoor and came straight through to the kitchen. Robertson carried a small cardboard box which he set down immediately. Conversation bubbled up briefly as Abney and King reintroduced themselves to their old mate Gifford; then Robertson, in his tireless dictatorial fashion, asked everyone to sit down so as plans could be quickly discussed. Pridell poured coffee and Robertson spread a AA road map on the parquet floor. He drew out a red felt marker and paused over the map. He glanced to King.

'Your in-laws own this place? Is it safe to stay in – for how long?'

'The old man's in hospital. It's okay for a week, maybe two.'

'All right. But otherwise I don't want you to group together – any of you. It's too dangerous. And we've already talked about alibis. Keep 'em up, keep 'em lively. Gifford's supposed to have been job-hunting in Southampton. He has a legit contact to prove that, no problems. Otherwise, no one's seen no one. Right?'

The group sipped coffee and agreed volubly. Robertson's attention focussed on Pridell. 'The snow is melting already, clouds not too bad. What do you think about that?'

Pridell's dreamy look answered for him. 'There's always the risk of delay but I'm not bothered. I think it should clear up, should be OK. Anyway, I don't think I'll be under too much pressure to move.'

Abney cut in, his voice lacking confidence: 'What about the top man? We should meet him.'

'He doesn't want that – and it suits us. What we don't know can't trouble us. For the moment I'm your go-between.'

'Are we assured the money – and the run out of the country if we want it?' King was draining his coffee.

'No worries there,' Robertson said. 'I'm quite sure he'll stick to his word. He hasn't got a reputation for double-cross. And he has plenty of friends who'll look after us if we go into Europe.' Robertson attempted a smile, a tight mouth-only effort that made him look ghoulish and scared. 'Anyway, I'll be riding close behind him to make sure everything is above board.'

'What about the cops? Who'll be on the job? Any of the friendly Old Bills?'

'I'd imagine someone like Havelock'll take the case. He'll probably ask for the RCS. The men there are Tate and Hackett. Hackett's got a tough record. Joined Uniform at eighteen, Divisional CID at twenty and fast through the ranks – you know the type. Some of my provincial friends speak highly of him. But our intention is to lie doggo and let 'em sweep over us. We're all nice boys. There's no reason for suspicion. Nothing linking us in the last eighteen months.' He cast an inquiring look around and everyone shook their heads. Deeply preoccupied, Gifford was staring out at the cakes of snow melting and sliding off the trees. Robertson threw his felt marker across and the gentle blow made Gifford jump. 'Stick with us,' Robertson said. 'This is all important. After today it might be awkward to compare notes.' Gifford sat up stiffly, nodding enthusiastically.

Pridell's newspaper with the scream headline announcing the arrival of the American President in London was lying on the table and Robertson now took it up and slapped it cheerfully. 'First things first,' he chimed. 'Our golden boy is in. Everything going as per plan there. He's in London all day and tomorrow at ten-thirty hours he touches down at Royal Pier. Our strike time is eleven-fifteen hours.'

'Are we all right for equipment?' Pridell said. 'You know what I asked for.'

Robertson hooked the cardboard box across and opened it. He began emptying its contents on to the table. 'Here we are: a few truncheons from the *Guardia Civil*, courtesy of a military friend, one police Smith & Wesson, one Walther, CS grenades, courtesy of the Grenadier Guards, Belfast, overalls for those who need 'em, gloves . . . oh, and Aeronautical Chart NW 50/5½ in case of delay.'

Pridell took the chart and eagerly spread it on the table. It had been a long time – too long – since he'd lingered over flight plans. It was going to be good being back in action.

A similar verve had captured the other members of the team. The President was in, the snow was melting, all the old boys were together and Robertson was issuing orders as cleverly and lucidly as if he'd never been away. Now it was just a question of catching the prize. And all that required was tight team work, co-ordination, military care. If a shadow of luck favoured them they'd be in clover.

Leaning over the AA map Robertson ringed three areas – woodland west of Aldershot, where they were now situated, a region just north of Winchester, and another east of Weston-super-Mare.

'Let's talk about tactics,' he said.

Abney interrupted. 'Before we go on with that, what about our target? Some details?'

'I almost forgot,' Robertson smiled. 'I brought you some picture books to study form.' He rummaged again in the box and produced some colour-printed leaflets.

The explosion of Louise's .38 revolver thumped into Hackett's ear like a physical blow. Twenty yards away a circular smudge splashed onto the canvas-covered target, a couple of inches below bull. The overhead Ventaxia fan whipped the wraiths of smoke away before they could bank and gather. Not for the first time in the years of their working relationship, as he approached Hackett found himself eyeing her in an admiring, yet ambivalent way. He watched her stance: the slender legs apart and braced for balance, knees straining the hem of the tightish skirt, arms outstretched, left hand supporting the right for aim. Her body looked pliable yet firm, the waist nipped by a broad leather belt, the breasts jutted splendidly forward. But the allure of the body was offset by the almost animal aggression of the face. Hackett had never known whether or not she filled the free hours of her life with passionate lovers and, if she did, he wondered now how she treated them: with the softness promised by her body, or with the dominant assertiveness reflected in her eyes? On another day he might have lingered over that thought, and taken advantage of the cloisteral quiet confines of the underground practice firing range at police headquarters to find answers to his questions. But not today. The impatience, the nerviness, the anticipation of a big job overshadowed everything. There was time only for preparations.

Abandoning the gun in a case of wax cartridges, Louise strode across the lined area to meet Hackett. 'Getting the flavour of it,' she said.

'You're out tomorrow – you know that? Front of the crowd position. You'll carry the Smith & Wesson.'

Louise nodded. It would be the first occasion in a year that she'd be armed. She wasn't looking forward to it. Few policemen do. There are too many risks and the cost of mistakes is far higher. In a crowd like tomorrow's, the dangers were multiplied incalculably.

'Job for you,' Hackett went on. He whipped a typed sheet from a bulky folder of notes. 'Fancy an afternoon in London?' Louise had almost expected the task. She read the addresses, saw they were all East End. 'Who?' she said.

'Abney. Want all you can get. Associates in the last few months, anything they might know about him, his plans – anything.'

'It's more a man's job,' Louise said reasonably.

'Not in Stan Abney's case. Two of those addresses I got from the Yard. Prostitutes. Great chums of his. He's a ladies' man. You can trump up something convincing if you're asking women 'bout him – say he ditched you, owes you money or something. Don't go in head first. Read the notes I've jotted down there."

'Right. How long have I got? Want me back tonight?'

'Um. That's the problem. Drive up now. Phone me if there's any break. You can drive back late, get some kip. We're too late to expect miracles, so the important thing is being ready in the morning.'

As Louise was packing her equipment away the door behind Hackett crashed open and Tate, looking harried and red-faced, marched in. 'They told me you'd come down. Not that desperate for a steady shot tomorrow, are you?' He gave a short humourless laugh. 'Fatalism was never one of your weaknesses.'

Hackett grunted.

'Any luck with the London investigations?' Tate avoided Hackett's face, as if preparing himself for bad tidings.

'Zero,' Hackett snapped. 'CRO files were out of date. The job info was wrong. We got back on to families and sorted things out a little, but we're no nearer. Abney and Gifford have gone into thin air. Gifford's mother hasn't seen her 'boy' since he went after a job as shipping clerk down here. No trace at all on Abney – despite the help of C-12. Robertson's mother claims her son quit his job as building site foreman and went north after another. Pridell has a wife and grown-up son. Dicey marriage. The wife says he's in trading, buying and selling dolls of all bloody things. Says he went to Spain for a business-cum-pleasure trip. Confirmation on his ticket, no reply from Malaga Immigration yet, but it looks sound enough. And King's wife – divorced – says he went to look after a sick friend. She was downright messy, refused to lend.'

'Paluzzi?'

'Nothing. I spoke to a couple of people who'd had dealings with him last time round. He had a friend, ran a haulage, shipping company – he might have been worthwhile but he's dead. For all the help I got otherwise everyone else might as well have been bloody dead. Nobody's heard from him. Everybody tells me he's retired, living in opulent nothingness in never-never land.' Hackett ambled casually up to the firing line and withdrew his revolver from his hip holster. He shook out the cylinder, checked the chamber and emptied out the five cartridges. A few wax stubs were lying about and he loaded these up. 'If it wasn't for the Flying Squad word – and then Gifford – I'd convince myself the Paluzzi thing was self-delusion.'

'Did you wire Interpol to see if they could help?'

Hackett mumbled affirmatively. 'All they know is that he's been dividing time between Berne and Paris. He's not in Berne now and they've no address in Paris.'

Tate took up the fat folder Hackett had laid aside and started to leaf through it. As ever with Hackett, the thoroughness of his record-keeping was impressive. The words 'State Visit' were neatly stencilled on the outside of the folder and page after page detailed past histories and current movements of every known target who might even remotely be associated with an assassination plot.

Taking position at the twenty yard line, Hackett levelled his gun. 'I've put a few people up to London to dig round, see if anything comes up on the Big Five. Hart's looking at Gifford's friends, Louise is gone up now to check Abney – each of the team will be chased up.' As he stopped speaking he fired rapidly twice. Two dead centre hits. He dropped on one knee and waited for the smoke to clear.

'What about tomorrow? Your boys ready?'

'I've arranged placings with Pemberton and Havelock. Looks all right. And I've sent my best men up to the Cheltenham range with a few Parker Hales.' He fired again, another well-lined shot. He turned back to Tate. 'And that's not fatalism,' he said. 'It's plain realism. If there is a hit being planned, it doesn't look like we're going to get in there on time.'

Tate's face darkened with the import of Hackett's view. He shrugged. 'We'll keep hoping,' he said. 'Something usually comes up.' He forced up a smile. 'And anyway, we're a lucky squad. We have a talent for falling on our feet.'

As Tate left the range Hackett primed himself for the last shot. He extended his right arm, clutching the wrist with the left and relaxing his shoulder muscles. The ramp foresight moved into line with the rear and he centred on the target in the alley. He flexed his right forefinger, tensed it – then pulled hard. Nothing happened. The single word of a misfire sounded, jaded and mocking. He jerked the gun up and rolled out the cylinder. He cursed loudly. There were three wax cartridges, not four. He had had his quota of shots.

In controlled rage he stomped out of the firing range. That kind of mistake made bad cops. And dead cops. In the back of his mind he blamed the distraction, the lack of concentration, on the gnawing thought of Paluzzi. It was an exquisitely plainful notion to think of him out there, somewhere in the city, like Hackett counting the minutes . . . but to what?

Burying speculations, Hackett went to search out Pemberton. It was time to reconnoitre the route.

Dink was uptight. As she stepped off the bus that left her on the outskirts of Putney, she paused for a few minutes, waiting at the stop, glancing repeatedly down the road.

It might have been imagination or coincidence, but, quite casually, she had seen that same face in three different places today. A good-looking brunette – no more than twenty-eight but dressed for thirty-five, a little too prim, too *classy*. She'd been in the corner shop early in the afternoon and the girl was there, browsing at the paperback stand; and two hours later, when Dink had started for home and called into the High Street supermarket – the brunette had been there too. Then, when she changed bus in Shepherd's Bush Road, she had been idly inspecting the passing snarled-up traffic and the face had materialised again – the brunette driving past in a Dolomite Sprint, a racy car Dink recognised because, once upon a time, Stan proudly owned one. Or at least *had* one.

In normal circumstances Dink would have passed the coincidence of the girl off lightly – she wasn't the fanciful type, wasn't even normally observant – but after the copper last night and the phone call from the stuffy woman who claimed to be a friend of Stan's, she had a disconcerting sense of something being very wrong. Stan had told her nail-biting stories of police investigation work and she wondered vaguely if it might just be possible that a big check-up was going on round her. But what could it be about? What could Stan have gotten himself involved in? She searched for an answer, recalling all their conversations of recent weeks, but came up with nothing. The reason for police interest was just as baffling as the reason for his vanishing act. She just couldn't unravel it.

She had thought the Dolomite was following her bus but now, five minutes after the bus had moved, there was no sign of it. The traffic currents were turgid and a string of large vans had blocked the junction turning into the road. If it was tailing the traffic knots had probably slowed it down. There was nothing to be gained by waiting to see if it showed up, Dink thought quickly; better take the opportunity to get home. She cursed Stan for absconding without as much as a hint of his intentions – or his troubles – and walked to her flat in an uncharacteristically fast half-trot.

Inside, she threw down her coat and kicked off her shoes. Emptying the groceries, she went through to the kitchen to make up some food; but she wasn't hungry enough and her breath was still whining in her chest from the rush home. For ten minutes she drifted restlessly round, moving from time to time to the window that looked down on the road, half-expecting to see the blue Dolomite; no car came. Then, deciding a bath and a cocktail would be the ideal mood-changers, she stripped off, ran her bath and went in search of the Gordon's.

So much of Stan's gear was littered around the place that it was impossible not to mull over this disappearance caper. One thing was sure, Dink told herself, if he *was* into something rotten, this time she'd have nothing to do with him. It had been bad enough with the girls he had been pimping. That was inexcusable really, but she was a softie for him and she'd surrendered quietly to his prolix apologies. The problem with Stan, she had always told herself, was that he had no control over himself. No sense. He didn't know when he had it good. He was a selfish man, she concluded now; and after all her kindnesses, he had little respect for her or her feelings. That was the real degrading part – the fact that, after all these months he could just take a mood and go, leave her without as much as a note.

She mixed her drink, took off her underwear and sank into a deep, sizzling bath. With the gentle ripples of relaxation fluttering up her legs and body, and the hot sting of the alcohol in her belly, she lay and decided, very coolly, that no matter what happened, the affair between her and Stan was over. If he tried to make amends in six days, or six weeks or six months, she'd tell him to bugger off. He wasn't playing the game by the rules.

The telephone started ringing.

She knew before she'd scrambled out of the bath and dripped her way across the living-room floor that it was him.

'Where have you bloody been?'

'Too long a story, love. I'm in Winchester now.'

'Winchester for Chrissake! Doing what?'

'Business. Good business. Couldn't get in touch 'cause we'd a lot to do.'

'Who's 'we'? What business are you doing?'

'Honest, honey. Leave it. I'll speak to you when I see you. Listen – ' His voice sounded edgy, blistering. He was in form for fight. 'If anybody wants me I'm doing a bit of long distance work – lorries, you know.'

'*I* want to know – to hell with anyone else – what are you doing?'

'Look. I said I'll tell you, didn't I? I'll be in touch over the week-end. Leave it till then. It'll be worth your while.' The voice had become truculent.

'That's not good enough.'

'I've got to go,' the voice interjected. 'Big day tomorrow, lot to be done. Look after yourself – okay? Keep my side of the bed warm.'

'Hold on a sec. I hope this job is all right?'

'Don't bother me, will you? I said I'll see you.'

The line was dead in her hand, purring loudly like the noise of her own thoughts. She put the receiver back in its cradle and sat on the sofa staring at it. The room was cold, March cold, and she was naked, but her body and face burnt with indignant fire. Frustrated tension held her rigid on the cushion's edge and riddles of sweat mingled with the bath water, running from under her arms.

The bastard was pushing his luck, manhandling her like that. He didn't give a damn! And he was up to something – something dirty. Her eyes jumped into focus sharply and she saw she was staring at the telephone message-pad. Stan had been doodling there and the address and number were still on the page – the address that had mystified her. Maybe that had something to do with his running off. Maybe she should say that to the police. She'd be getting back at him nicely if she blew the gaff on some trick he was planning. She stood up and went looking for her bag, for Hackett's number. Anyway, she told herself lightly, she'd be doing him a favour if she helped stop him.

Uncertainly she dialled Hackett's number. Abney's note with the address of *The Golden Gun* club was in her hand. She remembered him saying he had an important friend to meet there – that was days ago. When police headquarters answered and she asked to be put through to Hackett's extension, in a flash her uncertainty died. She was doing the *right* thing. If Stan was heading for trouble that nice copper might pull him out. She would be as helpful as she could. She would tell him about Winchester and about the important man at the club. And about the job tomorrow.

A thin voice crackled down the line. 'Is it specifically Superintendent Hackett you want, Miss?'

'Yes.'

'Sorry. He's not in. I can put you on to someone or take

a message.'

'Well . . .' Speaking to coppers always unnerved her. She plucked up courage, spoke strongly. 'No, doesn't matter. No message.'

'You might try later tonight or in the morning.'

'Fine.' Dink rang off and strolled back into the bathroom with Abney's note. On an impulse she tore it up and flushed the pieces down the toilet. To do what she had tried to do was stupidly spiteful, she decided – just the kind of ineffectual triviality that Stan would laugh at her for.

The best thing to do, she thought, was to wait until the week-end and see what story he came up with – wait and see if this business was as 'good' as he promised.

4

By nine o'clock on Friday morning the sun had broken through scudding clouds and was hanging like a brilliant lucky pendant low in the eastern sky. For the crowds gathering in the streets near dockland since eight, the sunshine put the seal on the promise of a truly glittering occasion. Factories and shops on the procession route had closed for the day and bus services were rescheduled and diverted from the area. Thirty major and by- roads were closed to cars and the men and women from traffic and uniform were out early, busily absorbed in keeping things tidy, ready and safe. Colourful bunting and roving bands of noisy children ignited a jolly carnival atmosphere and American flags rustled endlessly in the off-shore breeze.

A less inspired humour permeated the duller corridors of police headquarters. Force Operations Room had cackled, rang and roared with life all through the night and by dawn a cancerous spirit of defeat and disillusionment had won its way in. Every one of Hackett's fifty-man Squad would be on the streets for the duration so much of the night hours were taken up with briefing and discussion. But Hackett had been unable to mask the let-down he experienced. The principal of the terms of reference of the squad called for 'the detection and arrest of persons active in the commission of serious crime' and on that count Hackett had failed completely. He had had warnings and his sixth sense told him something was 'on', but he'd failed to isolate and curb it.

Havelock called a last-minute meeting with senior

officers and the FBI to clarify the position with regard to assassination information. Despite branch and squad inquiries, no reliable follow-up material had come to light. Pemberton thought now that his original informant had been misled and Hackett suspected diversion. There was always the possibility of an attempted kill, but Havelock personally felt optimistic. The US Secret Service had provided a few extra men and a total of forty-five armed men and women would provide long-range and crowd protection. Succinctly, Havelock reviewed Chief Superintendent Shaw's traffic arrangements and Hackett made a brief speech about the position of marksmen on the motorcade route and on the shared radio frequency in use by the Branch and Squad for the day. This meeting was succeeded by a series of talks to individual units, then everyone split up and the dress rehearsal began.

With five armed Squad members – Louise among them – Hackett drove directly to Royal Pier and, consulting Pemberton's Shots, placed each at a vantage spot on the narrow street that led into the pier. Then, using the UHF, he effected a swift exercise check to establish all positions. Louise, plainly dressed in a warm grey wool coat and a college scarf but with a gun slung to her hip, stayed with Hackett as he drove over the President's run for the last time. With the exception of police vans and two or three mobile VTR vans from the BBC, Hackett's Capri was the only vehicle left in the one-and-a-half mile run.

The streets rolled past, strangely stark and lifeless and Louise watched the boisterous groups on the pathways and wondered morbidly if, by evening, they would have as much to cheer about. As soon as the thought registered she shook it off as inappropriate for a policewoman. Hackett saw her moment of unease.

'How does it feel?' he smiled sardonically. She knew what he was talking about but chose not to take it up.

Hackett's chauvinism still forced him to make a joke of women with guns. When she didn't reply he slapped her thigh. 'Thirteen ounces of blood 'n thunder stuck in the waist-band of your knickers. Make you feel deadly?' She winked obscurely. The joke wasn't callous, she knew, it was meant to soften the air, comfort. His knuckles on the steering-wheel were white and his breathing was loud. The lack of success on this mission was really rankling. If today went badly wrong he wouldn't forgive himself, or the squad.

As they passed various buildings Hackett rattled out call signs over the UHF. Each of fifteen top marksmen – riflemen – concealed on rooftops acknowledged his message.

The crowds were thickening now, pouring into the streets, and somewhere nearby a brass band was striking up, tuning on 'Colonel Bogey'. Hackett said, 'We'll drive with the motorcade. You stick with me. Looks cosy. Keep up with the President's agents, right behind 'em. Okay?' Louise nodded. Crowd barriers blocked the road outside City Hall and Hackett's check was over. Swerving the car he accelerated off hurriedly and angled for the docks. Louise was tempted to talk, to ask him what he thought would happen, but she knew he wasn't in communicative form. Even last night. When she'd got back from London and reported the unsatisfactory results of her afternoon, with not one lead to Abney, he had simply shaken his head and said that was a pity. The momentum of events had him now, she knew, and his mind would be racing too fast for words. It would be unlikely that he would dally in chat for a day, maybe more – even if things went smoothly.

'There's the first 'copter,' he said. Louise craned forward, looked up. Like a silver bumble-bee, a solitary helicopter, droning loud, curved across the sky. As the sun glanced across it quickly the RAF legend painted on the side was clearly visible. Hackett looked at his watch. 'They're coming from the USAF base at Upper Heyford, so they should be in any minute. It's gone half-ten.'

The helicopter was swooping lower, beginning to stall and hover. As Hackett's car drew close to the pier the thunder of the blades filled the air. Louise rolled her window down and looked back into the northern sky. Immediately she saw the two following 'copters. A faint stir of life ran through the gathering street crowds. Someone started shouting. Louise told Hackett the Presidential flight was coming in. Following a cruising team of police motor cyclists, Hackett entered the pier area. 'Real danger is here,' he said. 'From the touch-down to the university and City Hall. If a gunman wants to have a go he'll do it while the procession is moving. Oswald-style. Do it when everything's in motion – easier for you to make a running getaway.' Louise opened her mouth to speak but he overrode her, flicking on the UHF and asking Price, one of the long-range Shots, if the parked patrol cars ahead blocked his line of fire from the top of a massive store house. Price replied negatively. 'Right,' Hackett rejoined. 'Get your trigger ready. Here we go!'

As the first 'copter touched down, away from the reserved and decorated space in the centre of the pier, Hackett pulled the Capri in alongside a rank of Squad and patrol cars. He jumped out.

The second 'copter, resplendent with its presidential eagle markings and freshly-painted underbelly, slewed over the dock storehouses and out over the pier. People began clapping and shouting and a thousand miniature flags appeared through the heads of the crowd and started bobbing gaily. Hackett watched the guard of honour, lined stiffly parallel with the marked landing area. Behind them, having calmly adjusted their instruments for play, the official military band divided its attention between music sheets and the skies. The crowd of on-lookers, wildly animated in contrast to the uniformed men, occupied one side of the pier, marshalled carefully together and corralled behind mesh iron barriers. Everything looked quite under control. For the hundredth time in three days Hackett surveyed the profile image of the near buildings printed on the shimmering sky. Nothing seemed amiss. One figure – a hazy silhouette – moved across the roof of the lumber stores. Hackett knew this to be one of Pemberton's boys.

The President's security men stepped off the first helicopter just as the second settled down. A hundred yards away across the pier Hackett could see Havelock and Pemberton move over to join the men. Then the President's craft was down and the spinning blades were slowing. A huge, atonal cheer soared up. The rush of sound shook Hackett momentarily and his right hand instinctively unbuttoned his jacket and touched the butt of the revolver. He felt his palms slightly damp. Two big men, State Department agents, edged open the second 'copter's door and hopped out. The steps were rolled up. The band leader called out an order and a resonant, cymbal-bashing tune began. Someone close to Hackett in the crowd shrilled out a discordant counterpoint, blaring on a trumpet. People were laughing and shouting. All eyes from the crowd were fixed on the yawning door of the second 'copter. Hackett felt a warm breath in his ear and the softness of Louise's body touched his arm. He jerked towards her. 'Everything okay?' he said tensely, unnecessarily. Louise was scanning the buildings opposite.

At last the President appeared. The responding cheer drowned the reedy strains of the band. The President paused on the 'copter steps, a bronzed middle-aged man with golden hair and an incongruous shiny ice-blue suit. He looked, Louise thought vaguely, like a caricature doll and not the real thing at all. Involuntarily, in the excitement of the moment, she stared at the man, her mind blanking to everything but the apparent unlikeliness of his glossy presence here in this tough grey little city. Hackett, beside her, gazed on too but apprehension and rigid alertness like a dark cataract blinded his vision. All he saw were mechanical pieces, paces of movement, numbers of obstacles, permutations, risk areas.

The Lord Mayor was greeting the President now and Havelock had moved up to join the US agents. The crowd noise had diminished. Hackett pushed past Louise and climbed into the car. He radioed base and asked if everything was clear. The reply came affirmatively. Louise craned in. 'Ready to get up behind the State car?' she said. Hackett nodded. 'That's phase one over anyway,' he said.

The band struck up the American National Anthem.

Price, the nearest of the squad marksmen on the store house at the pier's edge, set aside his Parker Hale and took up binoculars. Very slowly, like the pro he was, he scanned the pier and the streets surrounding. The only thing out-of-the-ordinary he noticed was the commotion at the wharf where the large ship had recently moored. He wasn't too surprised by this; during Planning Discussions Havelock had listed the security-rated traffic due on the day – one of the items, Price recalled, was due in from Piraeus. Crouching on the roof-top, huddled against the high breeze, Price tried to remember what that important booty was. He recalled Havelock shrugging it off as half-important but somehow it had seemed to him a little too special to be passed off so easily. He watched the ship through his glasses and wondered. If only he could remember what it was.

Like Saxons at war with the Normans, the basis of the constant civil strife between the 'underworld' and the state had always seemed fair and legitimate to Terence King. Born in Whitechapel, he had grown up amid the grime and the winos and the deprivation of the lower working classes.

The filth of his home had been tolerable for the first ten small years of his life, but then his eyes had opened to the world, he had discovered the fabulous opulence of the West End, just fifteen minutes away by bus. For a year or two, during the early stretch into adolescence, he had tried but failed to comprehend the ingredients that made his world so different from the glories of Mayfair. Then he discovered that money – and lack of it – was the common denominator. Here was the secret of life, the secret of youth, of cleanliness, of pleasure, of style. Simply money. The strata of rank and class failed to impress itself on him and he saw the world simply as a place where those who could battle for and win the cash, won also the freedom and happiness. Like the kids' games of earliest childhood, it became a straightforward issue of trying to win the castle back from the invading Normans. You used all you could – guile, force, everything. The ends always justified the means.

Terence King's great fortune had been, in his eyes, the meeting up with people like James Robertson and Stan Abney who saw the game in the same light. Robertson he particularly admired. Robertson possessed what none of the others had – a leader quality, and a sense of powerful imaginativeness. It had been Robertson who had delegated responsibility to the team, formed them, prepared them, developed their individual talents – and planned the worthwhile hits. Where he, King, looked after Transport, and Pridell was Technical Work, and Abney and Gifford were Muscle – Robertson was the brain. In a strange way, the failure of his most ambitious coup, the kidnap deal, had brought the team closer together. The years in prison had not lessened anyone's respect for his ingenuity and, when he had proposed this new hit, everyone had been co-operative. King had been openly enthusiastic. Always a man of action, a fighting Saxon, the two inert years had quelled his spirit. Now, at last, the spirit was burning bright again.

The only thing that bothered King, that slightly dulled his enjoyment of events, was the involvement of this Paluzzi fellow. Fair enough – King could appreciate the value of the kinds of inside information a man like Paluzzi could get. But he was a foreigner, and it didn't seem quite right, him pitched cn the Saxon side. And, as well, it didn't seem right running such a major job for – or with – a man you'd never even met.

These thoughts rambled through King's brain as he sat at the wheel of a stolen Rover in Valley Street, not far from the city centre. He had parked at 10.45 and there was still no sign of the promised truck. He was beginning to get edgy. The presidential thing would have well started by now, he knew, and there was a danger of delays caused by crowds. He would have to be patient. Lighting a cigarette, he climbed out of the car and examined his reflection briefly in the rear window. He smiled to himself. He looked convincing. The blue overalls and the oil-smeared cheek made him look like any other garage mechanic and the 'Running In' sign in the back window polished the effect. With casual interest he raised the bonnet and checked the sparks. He wondered how many curtains in the opaque windows of the terraced street around him were stirring in appreciation of his painstaking cover. 'That broken down car is still outside, Dad.' He could imagine the talk. He glanced at his watch again. Better not stall too much longer. Never wise to linger with false reg plates. On impulse he clambered into the car and drove on. This was the worst part of a job – the wind-up, the wait. There was only so much the nerves could take. You could be a tough-neck, the hardest man going, but inevitably the nervous system gets overloaded, you get rash, start moving too soon.

He braked the car, pulled in opposite a site under demolition. He checked the route map Robertson had drawn up with the Italian. Yes, he was still on course. His hand was shaking a little – a minute quiver that shook the fingertips only. He shrugged it off: excitement, not tension. Suddenly a scream tore into his head. On reaction he dropped the map, swivelled round. Across the road, down a narrow trade-entrance lane beside some factories, he could see through to a main street – Cannon Street, he thought. His heart galloped, then calmed. He could see people, a surging summer-coloured crowd, moving, weaving like worker ants. Of course! The procession! Cannon Street. He was forgetting locations. The President's car was approaching, en route for the university. If he moved the Rover back a little he could see the commotion clearer.

He edged the car backwards.

Yes – there was the motor bike escort, coming into the street. There were some private cars – probably Special Branch and the Squad. Any minute now the President would be here.

Just then the truck appeared.

King was leaning back, staring into Cannon Street through the lane. The flicker of sun on chrome caught the tail of his eye. He looked round. He tensed. Here it was – coming at last! Just as Paluzzi had said, just as he'd promised. A custom-built Ford armoured truck with no accompanying patrol. King laughed out loud. He swerved his head back, facing coolly up-street. The truck trundled past with an engine drone not unlike sweet, thrilling Wagnerian music to King's ears. He fired the Rover's engine and started after it.

For a short time he cruised close to its rear doors. The winged emblem of Safelock Security seemed highly appropriate for the day – the painted bird looked stately, fearless and victorious.

For ten minutes, through stodgy traffic piling up because of the President's diversions, King kept the truck in close sight. Then traffic thinned out and the slow run for the city outskirts began. Sitting humming songs to himself in the Rover, King surveyed the van keenly. There were two aerials – UHF radio, he knew. There would be four armed men in that truck, locked into the back compartment. From time to time the driver or his mate would radio the Safelock headquarters to report position. That was a danger point. Robertson had been troubled by that. But, in planning, all the eventualities had been thrashed out. Today, if everything went with the military ease hoped for, the task would be a walk-over. One truck and six men – too good to be true!

At the city outskirts King overtook the truck and roared northwards, making good time on the quietly-trafficked road. After a few minutes of fast motoring he pulled off the main road and drove to a pre-arranged AA call box. Getting out of the car, he rang a local number. Immediately, before the phone had buzzed twice, a voice answered:

'Yes?'

'Friend's here. On time.'

'Good.'

'All cars okay?'

'Did you enjoy the President?'

King spat through his teeth and rang off. That was Abney. Jocular and wry as always. That conversation had been planned, designed to sound nebulous. Trust Abney to flavour it with his own bravado jest. Some day that bastard would get himself in a lot of trouble by breaking laws – not civic laws, but the laws of his own kind.

Regaining the Rover, King headed back for the main road. The timing was accidental but exquisite. As he dawdled, awaiting access, the Safelock truck rolled past. King shouted out with satisfaction and accelerated after it.

The truck was a little late, but making up time on the drive. Everyone would be ready. The cars and the trailer-lorry would be set, waiting. The sun was shining and the weather forecast was excellent. The President was keeping the city happy – and busy. The odds were stacked, too favourably almost, on *their* side. It was certainly a day for celebration.

Traffic through the next built-up area was exceptionally free-moving. They were ahead of time now. King allowed himself to tail back a little, dodging into a broken stream of juggernauts for a while and coming back into action only when the Safelock truck cut into the fast lane and sped far ahead. With a few heavy darts on the accelerator he was back up with it, trailing not three hundred yards behind. Then – at last – the first green hoarding announcing turns-off to the motorway loomed up before them. King looked in his rear-view mirror anxiously. God, it was just too good! Not one car – *nothing*. Not that it would matter much if cars drew up – but the simpler things were, obviously the better.

Ahead, as plotted on Paluzzi's map, the truck signalled its intention to turn left, headed for the slip-road that led directly to the north-bound motorway. King rolled his window down and peered forward. Yes! Abney had done his work as instructed. A half-dozen yellow cones were placed loosely on the macadam hard shoulder, ready if necessary to block the end of the slip to further traffic. But now that looked superfluous. King's job was virtually a no-go. His end of it was just about over.

As the Safelock truck drove down the curling slip-road, the Rover pulled up and King stepped out, taking a police diversion notice from the boot. Running back along the road, he kicked a few of the cones across the end of the slip where it forked with another, more circular route. Then he positioned the sign which was prefixed 'Accident Ahead'. Still there was no sign of on-coming vehicles. He glanced back at his watch. He knew he had to hold this post for six minutes. From the leg-pocket of his overalls he withdrew a small red flag and strode out into the middle of the road.

Further along the slip the Ford truck motored round a tight bend and suddenly saw what appeared to be a skidded lorry blocking the road. There was a man lying, as if injured, on the ground below the cab. A car – a dark green Jag – was parked, aiming the wrong way. And there was another car on the grass bank.

The driver of the Safelock truck slowed down, his sensory system reacting before his brain had actively considered the scene. The brakes screeched stridently as the truck came to a halt. For a moment – a silent moment of utter stillness – the driver looked over the stopped vehicles, searching out damage, blood, movement. Everything looked frozen. Nothing, not even birdsong or the whisper of traffic, stirred the air.

In the back of the truck, sweating and chatting about the firm's forthcoming Easter holiday golf outing, the security guards paused quickly when the stab of brakes rocked the cabin. One man, the nearest, slid across the bench-seat and spoke into the grille connecting to the driving cab.

'Everything okay?'

'Sure – accident ahead,' the driver mumbled.

The man in the back flicked the grille closed. Then it happened.

A hulking figure – Abney – rushed out from behind the Jag, ran towards the Security van and swung something in his hands. The driver had a brief impression of a long wooden handle, and the grimace of strain on Abney's face. Whatever he was wielding weighed a bit. An ear-shattering crash followed and the front reinforced windscreen of the truck vanished into a million cracks, clustered together like half as many blobs of white paint. The driver's mate whipped out his Colt pistol. 'Raid!' he screamed. 'Get on the blower!' The driver pulled out his UHF phone. Scalding nausea was tickling his throat and his hand was shaking so much he could barely switch the phone on.

Outside Gifford and Robertson crouched beside the rear of the truck, hands joined. Abney, still brandishing his pick-axe, hopped up into their grip and was borne aloft. On the roof he turned to lend Robertson a hand, hauling him up. Robertson shinned forward swiftly, hefting a bolt-cutters. He grappled with the aerials, slammed the cutters twice and failed to snap off the wire. Abney screamed to him to hurry. Third time, the first aerial broke. He set to the second. Now Abney moved to the ventilator. As he had been told, it was a sturdy affair, an inverted cup of steel encircled by iron mesh with a fan inside. It was exactly what he expected. Two days ago he had climbed over a fence into a security firm's parking area and examined ventilator fittings on the vans. He knew where to aim, how much force to expend. Straddling the roof, legs wide, he smashed the pick into the side of the mesh, twisted, withdrew and struck again. In five blows he had the cap off. He looked down to Gifford.

'*Giff! Gas!*' Robertson had finished with the second aerial. His eyes shot to Abney. The bastard was using names! How many times had he told him to clamp up!? He barked an order to Abney.

Gifford threw the CS grenade up. Abney caught it, slipped the pin and dropped it into the torn hole. As he did a gunshot exploded out of the dark within, a close shot which skirted over his shoulder. 'Fire again and you're dead,' Abney called out. Through the rough wool of his balaclava helmet he could scent the acrid sting of the gas. Robertson had jumped off the roof now and, with Gifford, had drawn his attack truncheon.

As the CS took effect the plaintive coughs of the security guards inside became audible. Abney, still on the roof, had a Walther PPK 7.65 mm – Robertson's pet toy, a left-over from the Congo – and was covering front and rear doors of the truck. Repeatedly he screamed, telling the men inside to get out with their hands up.

After a minute the rear doors flew open. Gifford and Robertson stepped back, waiting for the guards to spill out. The vomitory stink of the gas blurred Gifford's mind for a second, making him feel weak-kneed, dizzy.

Then the guards started staggering out. The first two came, huddled together as if for protection, arms round each others' shoulders. Robertson pounced on them, lashing down well-aimed blows, knocking them to the ground effortlessly. The third slunk out Gifford's side and one hard sweep from Gifford brought him down too. The last man never showed. Robertson, holding a hand firmly over his mouth and nose, took a hurried glance into the cabin. The guard, he saw, had measured his length, out cold, on the floor.

'Right!' Robertson shouted. 'Let's get 'em in. You – ' Abney waved, 'watch the front. The gas'll get 'em too.'

Before he had finished speaking the front door shot open and the driver's mate, choking on the gas, tripped out. His gun was in his hand and he aimed vaguely at Robertson and let off two wild shots. Abney leant down from the roof and took aim with the Walther. 'Don't, you stupid bastard!' Gifford roared. 'Hit him!' Abney faltered, lowered the gun. Gifford rushed across and lashed out with his truncheon.

After his mate, the driver surrendered without resistance. Abney then dropped down from the roof and, with Gifford, quickly bound the men – hands and feet – and dumped them back into the truck. Robertson – now with the Walther – checked his watch. Five full minutes already. The CS had taken longer than he'd expected. And the aerials – he had only accounted for one – they had caused delay. They were running over. He shouted to Abney to hurry up.

Finally the last man was bound and thrown into the cabin. The stink of the CS had faded fast but it lingered still, enough to burn the eyes, to upset. Abney slipped his gauze mask on, mimicking Robertson. Together they scrambled into the rear of the truck, walking on bodies, falling over each other.

There were about twelve crates, all marked in foreign codes but with English language daubings appending each. Two were placed at the end of the truck, away from the rear doors and standing upright like new coffins in a funeral parlour. One was marked 'Boy', the other 'Kraters'. Robertson grabbed the 'Boy' and began hauling it towards the doors. At the same time he motioned to Abney to take the other crate.

Gifford had taken the wheel of the Jag now and reversed it close in to the rear of the truck. He opened the boot and, very gingerly, helped slide the wood 'Boy' crate from the truck down to the car. Abney followed suit with the 'Kraters' box. Gifford tried to close the boot, but the crates were too big. He called up to Robertson.

'Tie it down,' Robertson snapped. 'Time's up. We'll have to split now.' Already he was off the truck, working side by side with Abney, fixing the lock into a jammed position and using strong binding wires to keep the doors temporarily together. Abney slapped the doors. The job was over. He began trotting off.

'I'll take the lorry,' he shouted back. 'See you soon.'

Gifford watched him climb into the lorry that had blocked the slip-road and reverse back into position, aimed for the motorway. He turned to Robertson. 'Will I take the truck, dump it in the trees?'

Robertson shook his head. 'You take the Austin. I'll stick with the Jag. Before I go I'll move the Safelock up into the bushes – okay?'

Gifford agreed. He was glad to be going. The adrenalin

was draining out of his system and he was beginning to feel dried up, breathless. All that exertion was bad for a body so much out of condition. Had he more notice of the hit he would have trained himself, cut back on the booze, maybe done a little jogging. It had always been that way in the old days. He got back into the Austin parked on the verge, cast a final look at the raid scene, congratulated himself for a thoroughly professional day's work, and pushed into gear. As he drove away Robertson was nudging the Safelock truck up the steep roadside bank, into the elms that were green with the first buds of spring.

When Gifford was gone Robertson returned to the Jag, checked quickly over the road to make sure nothing incriminating had been left behind, then headed off.

He was just reaching the end of the slip-road – driving the wrong way – when the first car allowed through motored slowly past him. A young woman behind the wheel shot a malevolent look towards him – a half-second before she did he whipped off the balaclava helmet. He cursed King. The bastard had left his post early. Already the cones were gone, the sign – everything. That was the second mistake today. First Abney, with his impolitic shouting; now King with bad timing. They'd both take raps on the knuckles for that.

Taking the Winchester road, driving very fast, Robertson bleakly reviewed the hit. The slip-ups, he decided, were of minimal significance and it was very unlikely that the guards would be able to give any leads to the police. The woman motorist might be a problem, but she had got no more than the merest fast-moving glance at him. No doubt she might identify the car, but he'd be rid of that within the half-hour. Otherwise everything worked well. Faces had remained covered and no one got sick with the CS floating round. He had had doubts about Gifford's staying power, but the old boy had sailed through – and he hadn't half sallied forth with that bloody truncheon! A warm surge of satisfaction coursed through Robertson's veins. The empty road ahead of him, the speedometer touching ninety, the treasure in the boot. A good operation behind and good prospects ahead. This was the very essence of happy living: sound reliable mates pulling together, taking a chance, working hard to win. He was reminded of his early days of training, of his days in Berlin with the Royal Corps of Signals during the Corridor trouble. The discipline and challenge and harmony of those days set a precedent which had decided him on the kind of life he wanted to lead. He wanted to live under threat of war, with the spoils of war in sight. And now – in these last twenty years – he had lived out his ambition, extending it despite the agonies and soul-erosion of prison. Today's victory was a double win. Not only had he co-ordinated his men to take a priceless prize, but he had overcome the torpor induced by the lifeless waste of prison. There would be no going back now. The ten years in gaol – possibly as much as a fifth of a lifetime – would be made up for. From now on stakes would be higher, more risks would be taken. With top-class men like the team it would be wasteful *not* to remain operative. Soldiers need fight.

With these thoughts paramount in his mind – preparing his team for another hit – Robertson drove through Winchester. There was no unusual police activity discernible but he estimated it would be anything up to half an hour before the balloon went up. The likelihood was that Safelock's headquarters would become alarmed when no check-in calls came from the truck. They would immediately alert police and a few patrols would cruise the route to London. Then it was just a matter of luck, good or bad. The spot chosen for the raid on the truck was well concealed and the close forest of trees provided adequate cover for the truck. Suspecting a hit, a clever copper might deduce that just such an area, slip-road and all, would be an ideal place for a hold-up – and if that happened it was conceivable that the vehicle would be unearthed within an hour. But it would probably take longer. It was now 11.40. A fair reckoning, Robertson guessed, gave him till 12.45. By that time the treasure in the boot would be three counties away.

A further five minutes drive brought Robertson to the first signpost for Eastleigh airfield and he knew he was home and dry. With happy abandon he slammed his foot down on the accelerator. The needle on the speedometer hit a hundred, jerking onwards. Eastleigh no more than four miles away now.

A noise, a creeping, whirling noise edged into Robertson's thoughts. For a second he didn't recognise it – then his eyes closed tight and an iron hand flexed across his chest. He looked in the mirror. Jesus! They had him! Police! A car racing behind, the unmistakable blue-and-white, the flashing beacon. Confusedly he pulled back a gear, the car slowed, engine grating. He surged forward, back into fourth, ramming down on the pedal as hard as he could. King flashed through his head. Thank Christ for his mechanical flair! – the Jag was sliding along perfectly, topping over the hundred without as much as a wheel wobble. He could see in the mirror the police car was losing ground. Only then did he breathe easily enough to allow his brain to come up with an answer: they weren't on to him for the hit, nor for the treasure in the boot – they were after him because he was clocking up fifty in excess of the speed limit. He grunted at the irony. Now it was his turn for mistakes. Deadly mistakes. Even if they didn't catch him now he was in trouble. The stolen Jag would be traced, the link with the woman on the slip-road would be tied, the direction he was headed might be a giveaway . . . But no. It might turn out to be an advantage. *Stolen car –*

robbery car – spotted heading south. It would throw them all off the scent. They might think the stuff was bound for Southampton, for the boats. He smiled. But to do that, to mislead them, he'd have to shake the tail off before Eastleigh. If they connected the airfield with the robbery, then the heat would be on.

Still driving at almost twice the limit, Robertson swerved off the main road, bumped along a farm track, pulled back onto a by-road and tore on. The police Austin tried to follow, got temporarily stuck in mud on the track, lost a half-minute, then resumed the chase. Familiarity with the roads from studying area maps gave Robertson an advantage. The police, he knew, would be more used to principal routes and the larger by-roads so he stuck to more obscure tracks, choosing a circuitous run that would take him back to the Eastleigh road. Then an idea came to him. Ahead on a sleepy, forgotten little road an inactive-looking garage reposed quietly in the morning sun. Outside it, parked for repairs or sale, stood maybe twelve cars. There was no attendant in sight, no one. Free-wheeling down the hill, Robertson turned the Jag into the garage and rolled in among the parked cars. He manoeuvred slightly, nudging in as far as he could so that the rear of his car would be blocked from view of cars coming down the hill. He cut the ignition and waited. In seconds the police car appeared, hurtling down the hill, beacon still flashing. As it careered past he had a fleeting glimpse of two young profiles, capped men alive with the thrill of chase.

When they were a few minutes gone he reversed out, turned full circle and drove back up the hill. There was no time for hanging round now. The exchange would have to be quickly effected and the car would have to be ditched.

He made the Eastleigh road with no sign of the Austin and motored fast to the perimeter gate of the airfield. A pang of sudden uncertainty made him hesitate as he angled in. What if someone here saw the car and the woman's identification of it made the newspapers? A dark green eight-year-old Jag – how conspicuous would it be? Who would remember it at the airfield? How intensive would the police airport checks be?

The chance had to be taken. Pridell had waited long enough. It was too late to look for another car and anyway, hefting those boxes would be time-consuming, too awkward for one man. He looked carefully around, saw no one within a hundred yards of the gate and drove straight on to a line of squat buildings topped with a hoarding announcing the Viking Flying School. Pulling into a lane between two close hangers, he stopped, jumped out and ran to the open space beyond. Blessedly, there was nobody about. Six or seven light planes were gathered in a semicircle on a macadam strip that led to the main runways. The nearest, a Cessna 172 with a red-and-blue nose, had its door wide open and Pridell was sitting in the cockpit looking morose and tense. Robertson ran over to him.

'What kept you?' Pridell said gruffly. 'You nearly blew it. I've had pre-flight checks done, I've been kicking my heels. It looks bad.'

'Long story. Is everything okay? Weather?'

'Not too bad. Cloud, eight-eights at five thousand feet now – all go as far as I'm concerned. The stuff?'

'You'd best give me a hand with it.'

'Risky. A lot of people drifting round. I'll take it myself. I've more muscle than you.' Pridell hopped out of the Cessna and ran across the clearing. Robertson untied the boot and they hauled the two crates out together. One, the Kraters box, was considerably less heavy than the other. Pridell lifted this and walked the twenty metres across to the plane. He pushed it carelessly in and came back for the second.

'How does your pal feel about you borrowing his plane?'

Robertson said, closing the boot.

'He asks no questions,' Pridell smiled. 'Doesn't even know it's me flying it. Which keeps me happy.'

'Think you can manage?'

Pridell took the Boy crate in his arms and sidled off. 'Don't worry 'bout me. You just get lost, eh? Doesn't do to tempt fate. The boss of this Viking place is due back at twelve. He's gone into town to see the President, would you believe?'

Heaving the second crate into the Cessna, Pridell jumped in, waved and pulled the door down. As he started up he saw Robertson get back into the Jag and drive away. His blood sang. It was all up to him now. The ultimate move. The superb getaway. The brilliant end to a good job. He called Southampton Tower on his radio.

'Southampton, this is Golf Alpha Romeo Victor Charlie on one-one-eight decimal three. How do you read?'

The radio cackled. His mouth was dry. There was a cold beer in the haversack beside him on the seat. When he was airborne he could enjoy that. A flying victory drink!

Southampton trickled over the air. 'Golf Victor Charlie, Fives – go.'

'Southampton, Golf Victor Charlie is a Cessna 172 for Cardiff. One on board. My endurance is six hours and I estimate Cardiff at four-five. Taxi clearance?'

Tower gave him immediate clearance and he rolled up to the holding-point on runway Zero-Three. In a hurry, he ran through his pre-flight Vital Actions – trim set, throttle friction nut locked, mixture rich, carb air in cold, fuel on and sufficient, flaps set, checked. He went through the motions automatically, all the time thinking lovingly of the million-pound cargo in the space behind his head. It was good to be back, and back on a whopper at that. Informing Tower that his checks were clear and he was awaiting take-off clearance, the radio shook back into life.

'Victor Charlie, you are clear to enter and take off. Wind is zero-one-zero at ten knots, QFE one-zero-one-three, make a left turn out and call Southampton Approach on One-Two-Eight decimal Eight-Five.'

Pridell confirmed, adjusted and rolled out onto the runway. Then, without stopping, he rushed forward at full power, pushing the throttle right back and began a gentle take-off.

As the Cessna rapidly gained height he glanced down quickly and saw what looked like a blue-and-white police Austin drifting down the airfield road and turning in the Viking gate. It didn't linger. Driving once around the hangers as if looking for something, it moved back on to the road and headed citywards.

Pridell looked back into the vibrant blue sky ahead. His mind turned back to his cargo: a Greek treasure-chest of immense rarity. And immense value. He wondered briefly where the police would start looking for it and he guessed they would be – quite literally – a hundred miles off course.

With Louise and Bonney seated in total silence Hackett made the drive north in record time. The tip-off from Safelock had not come till 11.45 and soon after one the truck was located. Now, as Hackett's Capri swept down the slip-road, it was just gone two. The President had been in City Hall, lunching with the Mayor, and Hackett had been helping Uniform check out some deserted cars near the procession route when word came through. A security truck with valuable art work aboard had been hijacked and worked over. At first Hackett had not connected it with Paluzzi or his suspicions of the 'diversion' crime, then Tate had come along and told him Havelock had requested the Squad to take it up immediately. The pull was more than valuable art work, it was the priceless treasure from Ancient Greece, on loan from the National Museum in Athens and one or two other art centres. It had been bound for London, for temporary display in an exhibition of alloy and metal work. Hackett's first reaction to Tate's searing bluntness had been to ask, 'How much is it worth?' To which Tate replied, 'How much are the bloody crown jewels worth?'

Still unsure of the background to such a snatch, Hackett had got some details on the phone from local CID. The rough outline was enough to convince him the job had been professional, clever, and most probably Paluzzi's come-back venture. The President diversion had served its purpose exactly and Paluzzi had sauntered through a text-book robbery. Because he had more than half-expected it, Hackett wasn't particularly riled. Bonney detected and understood the ambiguous calm with which he received the news but Louise queried him. As they got into the car at squad headquarters she said, 'You can start shouting your head off, telling them you told 'em so – it looks like that kidnap team rebanded.'

'It's not them I'm interested in,' Hackett replied coldly.

'You reckon this is Paluzzi's league?'

'I bloody hope so,' he muttered with feeling.

'After his bad run here five years back?' Louise was questioning rather than disdaining. 'Lightning never strikes twice in the same place.'

Bonney chuckled. 'Um. And bad pennies have a habit of turning up again and again – eh? A good pro would have copped the value of the state visit a mile away. Specially in these circumstances, with treasure travelling. Ideal hit. Avoid the city 'cause that's where all the police movement is, let the treasure come to you. Choose your spot on a lonely country road and – pow!' He looked over to Hackett. 'Snatch job, just what the kidnap team'd be good at?'

Hackett was lost in thought. 'Just wait 'n see,' he said.

Two ambulances had arrived at the scene of the raid and one was still there when Hackett drew up. Crossing directly to it, Hackett asked the shaken security guards for their account of what had occurred. One man, the driver, was next to useless, gabbling nervously on, but another, a fat man with ugly weals from the truncheon attack across his neck and face, was helpful. Delaying the departure of the ambulance on Hackett's insistence, he gave a full account of the assault. When Hackett released him he joined the young CID Inspector sent out from Winchester who was supervising the sealing off of the area. Six uniform men assisted the task, diverting traffic to the alternative route. The pallid young man looked stricken with shock at the prospect of responsibility for the job. Hackett broke the good news, telling him the squad would be taking charge.

'What's been done?' Hackett asked.

'Roads blocked north, south, west. Nothing much east, but we'll set up the A31 as soon as we can. Problem is they've a massive start. We're looking for anyone who saw anything – regular users of the road, you know.'

Hackett nodded. 'Two cars – green Jag, black Austin 1800 – right? And a trailer lorry, grey, no markings?'

'We're checking them for thefts. Nothing in yet.'

'Anything from traffic? Anyone see the cars?'

The Inspector shook his head. The sullen look said he didn't expect the cars to be seen ever again. Somehow neither did Hackett – cr at least not for quite a long time. He walked back into the middle of the slip-road and tried to imagine the heist taking place. Guns, truncheons, CS, three vehicles – clearly the job was a sophisticated caper, carefully planned and expertly executed. The chances of substantial leads were slim. Acting on the premise that time buries crime, the robbers would be intent on concealing anything that might advance police pursuit for as long as possible. The cars used would probably be dumped in disused garages, or even resprayed and passed on. The one problem might be the lorry. Unless it was a case of someone knowing someone in the transport business, at which event the 'borrowed' lorry might be casually returned and never located. After that, the breaks would depend on eye-witnesses.

Louise came up with a bright expression on her face. 'I suppose we begin by asking what we're looking for – this Greek stuff.'

'Don't ask me,' Hackett barked. 'No doubt some egg-head'll tell us. Probably Cleopatra's chastity belt.'

'Ancient Greece – Cleopatra! You're a civilisation and a couple of hundred years out, I'd say.'

Bonney had been chatting to the Inspector at a patrol car. Now he came running over. Hackett could see the inspector talking rapidly into his radio.

'Good news,' Bonney said. 'Two reports on the Jag. Motorist saw it here at eleven-thirtyish, driving along the bank, wrong way up the road. District nurse – stopped at a check point and told the story. One man in it. Dark, big. That's it.'

'So it was headed – where – west, south?'

'South,' Bonney chimed. 'At eleven-forty-eight a patrol car spotted it, doing the ton down near Eastleigh. Gave chase but lost it.'

'Sure it's the same one?'

Bonney nodded. 'The woman gave half the reg, said she memorised it 'cause she was going to report it. Dark green, one man – it's close enough to count.'

'Driving south,' Hackett repeated thoughtfully. 'Now, where could they have been going? The docks?'

'I'll get on to it,' Bonney said and he ran back to join the Inspector.

Hackett walked back up through the elms to examine the Safelock truck. He was up on its roof, checking the smashed ventilator fan when a howling whine from the sky shook the birds out of the trees. He looked up. A helicopter, one of the Presidential trio, was gliding fast northwards. Hackett saw the time was gone three. The presidential trip was over. The decks were cleared. It was just two jobs now: Paluzzi and this snatch business. And the more he thought of the latter, the more he guessed those two tasks were one.

5

A short, unhealthy-looking Greek with brilliantined black hair and a bulky vicuna sweater bulging under his expensive silver-grey suit sat opposite Tate and said, in perfect English, 'There's no question about it, the property must be recovered.'

Tate inhaled sharply, rubbed his eyes and squeezed the bridge of his nose. To Louise, seated with Hackett on a desk-top in the corner, Tate seemed to be willing the little man to vanish. It had been a long, gruelling day. Nerves were frayed now and the deadly lethargy that accompanies anti-climax had set in. The inevitable had happened and this bombastic foreigner had been despatched down from the Greek Embassy to tell them why it shouldn't have happened. Hackett alone, Louise observed, was cool, alert, interested. The other two officers present, Gavin and Bonney, were too busily absorbed in their mugs of tea to express any involvement in the conversation.

'May I tell you, in a nutshell as they say, what exactly has been taken?' the Greek said gravely. 'Firstly, there were six items – all stowed in one light steel case within a wood crate – these were kraters and bowls of bronze, not only from Athens but from the Archaeological Museum in Thessaloniki. They include the famous bronze and silver krater from Derveni in Macedonia which is one of the finest examples of Greek metalwork from the fourth century. Indeed, probably *the* finest surviving. It is, need I say, beyond value. The other items in this crate are important, but the Derveni is irreplaceable.'

'How big is it?' Hackett asked.

The Greek took out a packet of Xanthi cigarettes and offered around. Only Gavin excepted one, and he quickly choked on the flavour and stubbed it out. The Greek rambled on:

'The Derveni is so high –' He made a measuring gesture with both hands, 'ninety centimetres, half the height of a man almost. The others, the bowls, are small. But – ' His face became melodramatically insistent, ' – in understanding and appreciating the Greek culture these items, every one, are vital. More than anything, the Bronze Boy is vital.'

The Greek paused reverently at the mention of the words and puffed quietly on his rich-smelling cigarette. Hackett said irritably, 'What's the Bronze Boy? A statue?'

'The supreme treasure of Greece. The best sample of Late Classical art certainly, dated at about 340, pulled up from the sea off Marathon. It's known widely as The Marathon Boy and it is especially important since less than a score of Greek bronze statues are left in existence. Throughourt the ages much of Greek art was ravaged, spoiled. In medieval times marble was at a high premium as raw material for lime, so all the marble statues were destroyed. Similarly with bronze. It was valuable as scrap and plunderers dug everywhere looking for it. The few pieces that did survive were usually dredged up from the sea – like The Marathon Boy – and these are the world's only solid links with a marvellous civilisation.'

'We'll want pictures of these things obviously,' Hackett cut in. 'What size is this Marathon Boy? How heavy?'

The little man seemed mollified by Hackett's flat enthusiasm. 'The Boy stands 1.30 metres, very recognisable, right hand extended above the head. The statue is hollow and the box is quite slender. I should imagine it would not weigh very much, but I can get the actual figures quite easily.'

'Good. Do that. And pictures. Sooner the better.' Hackett paced the room, hands buried in pockets. 'So we have two steel-lined crates, both, say, almost chest-high and not weighing excessively much. Where would they fit? Into the boot of a large car? Yes. Maybe a few small modifications to the boot, deepen the base – no problem. And the patrol that tagged the Jag said the boot wasn't properly closed – possibly crammed with something but not too low on suspension.' He swivelled to Tate. 'Fair to assume the Jag was carrying this gear, I think.' Tate shrugged.

'What about the boats?' the Greek interjected. 'Your CID people told me on the phone from London that you'd be checking the docks.'

'That's a possible,' Hackett said. 'We've men there now, poring over export lists and looking at warehouses. We've already checked out-going boats. Only two went out in the time between twelve and two. There were long hold-ups because of the state visit, affecting traffic. Of the boats that went out both have been cleared. One came back to the careenage dock with engine trouble anyway. The other, a P & O liner, had a thorough going over by Dock Police. And we're still looking. But the field is wide open.'

'I suppose we must presume it's a ransom theft?' the Greek said unhappily.

Tate got up, set down his empty tea cup. 'We'll look at every possibility,' he sighed wearily. 'No ransom demands have been made yet, but that's not too unusual. We call this the settling-in period. The robbers, whoever they are, will be waiting till the dust settles, waiting to see how we play it. Will we publish names of suspects, will we shake up anyone's family, will we go rough or lightly?'

'Sounds like a game for children,' the Greek said feebly.

'Oh yes,' Tate returned. 'Strategy, gamesmanship – it all counts. Like commercial warfare. It's give and take. Use your wits, try and out-think . . . .'

'Only vie when the vying's good,' Hackett said smilingly, quixotically. Gavin chuckled and Bonney chipped in with a jocular remark. The Greek blinked, appalled by the levity of the men whose job it would be to recover the best treasures of his country. 'Have you any suspects at present?' he asked coldly.

'Several,' Tate said reassuringly. 'And we're on to a good line of pursuit. If it's not ransom, chances are it'll be a sale – that the, er, goods were wanted by someone to sell to someone else, if you get my meaning. There are plenty of rich men, lunatics, who collect this kind of thing as a status hobby. The other alternative is insurance.' Tate's eyes had been drifting round the room, absent and obscure, and now they levelled, icy and unwavering, on the Greek. The man sucked hard on the Xanthi and coughed.

'Indeed, indeed. Do not think the Embassy hasn't considered this. We are investigating the insurance situation – but, need I say, with material of *this* sort, the policies will be quite straightforward, set by the museum trust and the government. No individuals will be involved and I don't think there would be any ground for that kind of double-cross.' The man shifted disconsolately in his chair. Tate enjoyed the respite, throwing the ball back into the Greek's court, upsetting his offensive technique. With a loaded, vaguely menacing stare he stood up and the Greek, defensively, instantly followed suit.

'Tell your Embassy people we are doing all we can. We are following some definite lines of inquiry and may have news soon. After that, we would appreciate your co-operation, specifically to Mr Hackett here, who will be spearheading the investigation. Photos, anything he'll need.'

The Greek extracted a few typed notes from his brief-case and handed them across to Hackett. 'All I've already told you is here,' he said. 'And I'll get weights and what-not later. I'll phone you with the facts. I'll see to pictures immediately and – ' He turned back to Tate, ' – I'll supply a full account of the insurance situation before tonight.' Tate opened his mouth to speak, to take advantage of the Greek's retreat and rub salt into the wounds; he decided to refrain – it was conceivable he would need favours from the Greeks before the case was closed. Politely he thanked the Greek for driving from London, promised to keep in hourly touch, then personally walked him to the lift.

When the door closed behind them Hackett jumped into action. 'Right, let's get back to the Incident Room. Bonney, Gavin – I want you back with Dock Police this evening. Visit any of our old friends down along the front. Sniff round. Find out if anyone was looking for a safe house, or shipping. Old Ezra the shifter, he might be able to help. After we busted him for the dope run he's had nothing but bad luck, he's probably looking for merchandise to move. After that we start surveillance shifts.'

'What have we got so far?' Bonney asked. His afternoon had been spent in company of two squad men combing wharfs and warehouses along the dockland. On arrival back at headquarters he had had time only for a shrink-wrapped sandwich from the canteen, then Tate's call to join him in his office had come.

'I got what I could from the security guards, but it comes to nothing. A good hit, savage and quick. Probably our old pals from London, the Five. No one saw faces but physically, in build, they tie up. Uniform are killing themselves looking for the cars, but nothing's come up. We can only guess where the goodies might be. No doubt they're unloaded somewhere safe, but that could be anywhere. Nothing to shout about at the scene of the raid. George from Fingerprints is doing a hundred-per-center, but nothing's come up. A Doctor Noble from the Yard Forensics Lab was called in by Havelock, but he's orbiting somewhere outside Pluto. On hands and knees in the truck, trying to sort out boot prints. Impossible task.' He sighed. 'Still, you never know, could give us a court case some day.'

'Have you got back on to families of the London team?'

'I sent Chick and Lennie up. Nothing. Everything as was. No Abney, no Robertson, no anyone.'

On the second floor, beside Hackett's Intelligence Bureau, an Incident Room had been set up in which Force CID and Squad men were working together, sifting through and collecting information piling in from fifty different sources. The spacious area, asthmatically hot with central heating blazing and twenty-five fast-working, sweating bodies blustering and bumping round the place, had something of the atmosphere of a Saturday afternoon bazaar. The discordant buzz of argument broke through a constant hum of phone conversation. Pausing only to check a new Interpol telex on Paluzzi (which proved still negative), Hackett strode across to a fine-scale wall map of southern Britain. Road-blocks were marked with red-tipped pins, the site of the raid with a black 'X'.

With Bonney, Louise and Gavin clustered round him, Hackett examined the map. 'If it's Paluzzi with the old gang,' he said, 'they're still here. He won't try the boats. Not yet. I'm sure he'd be too shrewd for that. The stuff will be comparatively easy to hide, but he'll want to be ultra-safe with it. A house in the country is out. Too obvious, always falls first under suspicion. Best alternatives are – one, get it as far away as possible; two, get in into the city, lost in semi-detached suburbia.' He took up a piece of chalk and marked the map. Robbery here, north of Winchester. Car spotted here, fifteen miles south, near Eastleigh. Almost a two-hour start.' He stretched an arm up, drew a rough scrawl over the top of the map. 'Could have got anywhere really – two hours, hundred and fifty miles.'

'But would they chance the roads for so long?' Louise

chewed a pencil, musing.

'Bright girl,' Hackett smiled. 'No, they won't chance that. They'll have given themselves a half-hour, three-quarters at the most.' He scribbled another chalk line. 'Which gives us this radius, say from Gloucester to Harrow with all of the south-east.'

'Marvellous,' Bonney chirped. 'London. Into the city and good-bye forever.'

'Not forever,' Hackett said softly. 'Not Paluzzi. No vanishing tricks, not this time. I'll bloody make sure of it.'

The door opened and Havelock strolled in, his eyes unnaturally dilated, fierce. He approached Hackett with a sheet of paper held out in front of him like a letter from heaven. His face glowed appreciatively.

'I spoke to the Safelock people,' he said. 'Mixed news. For starters, their driver's been released from hospital, come down to earth at last. They'd had him under sedation. He remembers bloody little from the raid. But he recalled a name – one of the men shouting to another. The name, he recollects was Tiff, or Giff or . . . .'

'*Giff.*' Hackett snapped his fingers. 'Got 'im. Bastard! He was in, then. Gifford. If it was him we can as good as count the others along too.'

Havelock smiled. 'Knew you'd like that. Hats off to the squad for working that one so confidently.' His smile diminished. 'The other snippet is, one of the security men has been rushed back to the infirmary. Intensive care. Suspected brain haemorrhage – result of a crack on the skull.'

'Christ! Chances?'

'Very slim. Doctor I spoke to said he's not rallying at all. They might try to operate.'

One of the FBI men from Grosvenor Square knocked at the door and pulled Havelock away to thank him for co-operation on the state visit. Hackett crossed to the window that looked out onto the night-time city to meditate on the new developments. A vicious aggression inspired by and aimed at Paluzzi and his reckless team held him immobile like a stone fist. Paluzzi, as ever, possessed the ethereal qualities that had assured him so long a life on the run. But the rest of the group were human, tangible. Through them, he knew, he could get to the Italian. And now he could run them down for more than robbery – for violent assault, possibly murder. But he'd have to be cautious, take them by the roundabout route, give them rope. Where would he begin? Gifford's mother? The girl Dink?

Someone touched him on the shoulder and he was jerked back into reality. White powder spilled from his balled hand, over his jacket. In his trance he had crushed the chalk almost completely to dust. One of his junior men was staring cheerily at him.

'Forgot to mention, Mr Hackett, call came for you. Last night. You were out with Pemberton. A girl. Seemed anxious to talk at first but then . . . .'

Late on Friday night, having dumped the Jag amid the garbage of an old fully-worked quarry and picking up another stolen van King had positioned there, Robertson drove east along the M4 in jubilant mood. The van had an old radio fitted (a nice thought of King's?) and he had been just about able to pick up Radio Two's five o'clock news summary. Police were acting on the theory that the stolen treasures had been shipped out of the country, it said. Intensive inquiries were underway in Southampton and other major south-east ports and the Greek Government had emphasised that no stone should be left unturned in the search for such 'historic arts of beauty'. The only thing that brought a shadow of frown to Robertson's brow was mention of the fact that close checks were being made at rail terminals and airports, as well. But, he consoled himself, that was a logical move and, with Pridell's elaborate cover plan, there would be nothing to link anybody with Eastleigh and, there again, the plans had been doubly-secured so that if the team *was* traced to Eastleigh, the route of the treasure would still be protected.

Turning off for Newbury, Robertson drove at his customary fast pace until he reached the first suburbs of the town. Then, turning back and re-tracing his drive to make sure no suspicious cars were following, he diverted northwards and motored to a small high-fenced yard at the end of a straggling country lane. The chicken-wire gate was padlocked, but Robertson produced a key and let himself in. Inside, in a littered, half-covered square two lorries, a Scania III and a Volvo, without trailers, stood parked. Between them, its roof glittering like diamond dust in the moonlight, a Mercedes Benz was parked. Robertson moved straight through to the two-storey stucco-and-brick building that abutted onto the yard. He gave a two-two-three rap on a door marked 'Whiteline Trunking Company', let himself in with another key, traversed the darkened hallway and went up one flight of stairs.

A fan of light spread out under one door on the landing and he pushed through, paused and gulped hard, catching his breath in awe and surprise.

Paluzzi was sitting in a leather office chair, side-on to the door, his profile immediately reminiscent of the Roman faces on ancient coins – angular, insolent, infinitely relaxed. His eyes didn't move towards Robertson and his gaze was fixed lovingly, passionately, on a dull, gleaming figure poised in the middle of the room. Familiar with the sleek shape from magazine pictures, Robertson was still struck, benumbed by the grace and beauty of the statue.

'You're late,' Paluzzi said softly, his attention still directed to The Marathon Boy.

'I check the airfield at Halesland. Just want to see how much we're ahead of the law.'

Paluzzi didn't reply for a moment, then took out a cheroot, lit it and exhaled a thin shaft of smoke. His eyes drifted off the statue. The spell was broken.

'Did everything go all right?' Robertson asked.

'Pridell did well. Made good time to Halesland – thirty-five minutes. He dropped from 2,500 to 800 feet to keep under Cardiff's radar, then took my signal and landed. I collected the treasure and he took off again – all very organised and calm. Pridell is a good man.'

'I only work with the best.' Robertson was aware of an almost hostile note of challenge in his own voice. In a back chamber of his mind he admitted to himself for the first time that, in a small way, he was afraid of Paluzzi. Paluzzi's brash manner and his confidence didn't unnerve Robertson, but the ingenuity of his mind could be intimidating. While Robertson had the men – and had a certain talent for stage-managing them – Paluzzi was the supreme director of affairs. The plan to steal the treasures had been all his, the information on Safelock, on the state visit, on routes – that had all come from him. Even the flight plan, to set a plane off for Cardiff and have a collector waiting with a car at Halesland, the small training field at the halfway mark – that had been his. And it had been devilishly clever because heavily controlled air space had been avoided and trackers in London, Cardiff or Southampton would have no reason to suspect a light aircraft had slipped under radar and stopped for ten minutes there. It seemed to Robertson a particularly brilliant way of shifting the takes without the danger of road-blocks, and getting the stuff *out* of the police net. The idea for it had been conceived by Paluzzi, Robertson recalled, in three minutes flat, over a week ago at their first proposal meeting.

'I admire the thoroughness of your work,' Paluzzi said.

'I take it everything was all right at Halesland? Good. And the rest of the team? Where did they go?'

'They all have various alibi covers, as we spoke about, and they've gone back to working them. I doubt if the law will have anything to bother anyone about. The hit was beautifully done, clean as a whistle. Once we all stick to our stories, we'll be fine.'

Crossing to the statue, Paluzzi caressed the smooth bronze arms with a kind of sexual gloating distorting his face. He tapped the second crate lying on the floor with his heel. 'It would be silly to borrow such a splendid fellow – and the kraters – and not strip them for the pleasure of seeing 'in the flesh' – no? I couldn't resist it.'

'It's . . . very good, very human-like,' Robertson said lamely.

'So it should be. It's supposed by some people to be cast from a human model. By the end of the fourth century in Greece, according to Pliny, sculptors were using real people to make their casts.' Paluzzi halted quickly, glanced disparagingly at Robertson, seemed to decide his erudition was wasted on a coarse-tongued rough-neck from the East End. 'Anyway, it'll fetch the figure I'll be asking for – no trouble at all. It, and the kraters.'

'You've heard the radio news? The police are checking airports, boats . . . .'

'Let them. Fruitless errand.' His brows raised, as if in query.

'True,' Robertson agreed. 'Do we keep it all here?'

'Safest place. Under my eyes, and while you're here for the week or so, under yours.'

'Roads around here are very quiet.'

'It's the answer to a dream. When I chose it I didn't really consider its suitability for this sort of thing, but I must admit it brought itself immediately to mind.'

'When it's . . . all over, will you base yourself here or in your, er, main company?'

Paluzzi regarded Robertson unspeakingly for a minute, the eyes quite dead in the centurian face. Behind the eyes the brain was pacing fast. Paluzzi needed sound allies if he was to make a good go of it in Britain. The Robertson team had proven its professionalism before, but they had hammed up the last major job; yet, despite that, he trusted Robertson, believed him to be a dedicated man whilst not understanding any of his motivations. Should he take Robertson more fully into his confidence? Tell him about the bankrupt company he had purchased in the Isle of Man? About his setting up there as a low-profile import-export trading agent? About all his future plans? His better judgement, gleaned from thirty years in crime, told him never to put more faith in associates than one absolutely *had to*, but equally he knew working totally alone was not feasible. And, if one was forced to choose, one could do a lot worse than this Robertson, with his cunning imaginativeness and his ruthless style. Involuntarily Paluzzi shrugged his big shoulders.

'This 'Whiteline' company is only rented by me,' he began softly. 'A retired Sicilian, old family friend, used to run it. He sold it out two years ago and it has been under threat of closure ever since. Man who bought it is old, no more interest in trunking, lorrying, transport. My Sicilian friend put me on to it, said I should buy it as a step into Britain. I was in two minds. So I came to a lease agreement with the old man.'

'Is he – the old guy – safe?'

Paluzzi laughed a little. 'You've a tendency to the dramatic, my friend. Of course it is safe. I'm a legitimate businessman – Ian Bryant – of Italian parentage, naturally. I'm interested in opening up in a big way here but want to run the field first, see what business methods are like, use my contacts and try out my techniques.' He crushed the cheroot out on the floor. 'For the last eight weeks, as you know, I've been exploring the market here, finding my feet as you say. I have begun to like what I see. The transport business appeals to me. Nicely vague. Your business is on four wheels and capital outlay is slight. I might – ' He paused, moved up close to Robertson and stared him defiantly in the eye. 'I might stick it out here. Not personally – but I might keep up the lease, run a few trucks. I could overlook operations from my own base. And I'd put a sound man in here to take care of this end.'

Robertson knew what was coming, didn't know how to evaluate it, didn't want to try now. He sat down, lit a cigarette and brusquely changed the subject. 'What about my men – if they want to go to Europe with their cuts in this haul? You'll look after it?'

'By all means, my dear boy. I always fulfil my promises. Your men are good. I won't let anybody down. Twenty grand each was my offer, and so it shall be. In a day or two.'

A sonorous bleating, muffled but close, stopped Paluzzi in mid-sentence. It sounded in three short jars, then silence settled again. Robertson saw Paluzzi's face pale in fright. 'What was that?' he hissed. 'Did you close the gate? Is it a car, in the yard?'

The noise came again, followed by the muted slam – quite clearly – of a car door. 'Were you followed?' Paluzzi shot. 'Who knows you came?'

Robertson shook his head, certain of his clean arrival. He moved quickly across the room and cut the light. Below, from the yard, the sound of heavy footfalls on gravel were audible. A dry lock squeaked. A foot scuffed the boards of the hallway.

'Hardly the bloody cops,' Robertson whispered. 'Trumping the horn?'

A voice spoke, high-pitched and blunt. The bang of a closing door covered the words. Silence followed, then the tip-tap of steps on the wooden stairs began. The landing light was switched on, its softened glow pouring, orange and ominous, under the door. Robertson saw Paluzzi move in the shadows, saw him pull something off the wall, heard a fluttering swish, as if a sheet was being spread on a bed.

Then, from very close by, on the landing, a voice – a woman's voice – said, 'Are you here, Frank? Frank?' Breath whistled gently. 'I saw your light from the yard. I saw your car.' The doorknob twisted and clinked. As the door swung in Robertson saw the slim figure of a tallish woman thrown in relief against the landing window. The scent of her expensive perfume rushed into the room. Then the light snapped on. Paluzzi had crossed to it and now stood, just inside the door, his face severe, drained of its deep mahogany tan. 'Why did you come here?' he barked. The violence in his tone was unmistakeable. 'How did you find me?'

The girl, Robertson saw, looked dewy-eyed and slightly drunk. Her jaw hung open and a brazen, haughty look made her pretty face unattractive. She walked unsteadily into the room and took a chair. 'Knew you'd be happy to see me,' she said mockingly. Only as she sat did Robertson notice the statue had been covered, draped in the darkness by Paluzzi with a coat from the antlered stand. Paluzzi towered over her. His petulance was sharply brought under control. 'You followed me?' he said easily. 'When?'

'Yesterday,' the girl said sluggishly. 'When you left the club. I thought it fair. If something is happening I should know. After all, you're involving me. And before, in Milan – ' She pulled up abruptly and looked at Robertson. 'You,' she pointed. 'I saw you at the club. You're doing business, eh?'

Paluzzi beamed a sudden smile and sat in his office chair beside the girl. 'This is Serena,' he said quietly. 'A great help to me in days gone by. And still a great help to me.'

He took one of her hands in his. 'Why didn't you call in yesterday? If you drove all the way up?'

A scowl furrowed the girl's brow. 'I dunno. I wasn't sure.' Her tone was blatantly suspicious and her eye had set on Robertson. Alarming accusation was in the look. Robertson turned away. 'So tonight, being my night off, I said, what the hell. There was nothing doing and I was going to drive up and see my sister in Reading. So I decided I'd call here. Then I saw the car.'

Paluzzi laughed dryly. 'You had a few drinks and you came up, yes?'

Serena giggled harshly. 'I'm not afraid of you, Frank,' she said. 'We – you and me – we're too old friends. I ran the errands for you in Milan and I'll do it again. You and me.'

With apologetic ease he pulled her up from the chair. 'Please, my dear girl. Not now, not here.' He tossed a glance to Robertson. Gripping her firmly round the waist, he guided her to the door. 'Come now. We'll go into town and have a drink together. Best place to talk about business, yes? And I'll tell you my plans.' He left her on the landing. 'You go down and wait in the car. Too cold here. I'll be down in a few minutes.' He winked importantly to her and kissed her cheek placatingly. After a moment's uncertainty, she acquiesced and moved off.

Mounting rage contorted his face as he walked back into the office. Serena had upstaged him. Her intrusion was the first development he had not accounted for. She had him in a corner now. There were no choices of movement for him; he would have to tell her his operational plan. If he didn't she would plague him – maybe too dangerously. Women, he had learnt sorely, were fickle creatures. When they suspected you of deceit you had only two options: come clean or run.

'She guesses you did the treasure snatch,' Robertson

said flatly.

Paluzzi fought to contain his irritation. 'Yes, maybe,' he mumbled. 'She's an intelligent girl. Maybe she heard it on the radio and added up the facts.'

'You shouldn't have used her, the club . . . .'

'I needed a base close to the city,' Paluzzi half-shouted, his face darkening. 'The plans were hurried. You knew. I needed a safe house and I saw no reason to mistrust her.' His anger burnt out swiftly. 'Anyway,' he sighed. 'She'll be no extra risk. A good girl.'

'She saw the statue, the boxes with Greek writing.'

'No she didn't.' Paluzzi's voice was a command, not a conversational comment. 'Like I say,' he grumbled on, 'there's no danger in her knowing. There's no link to me through the club.'

Robertson felt suddenly anxious. An insidious uncertainty he had never seen in Paluzzi before now radiated from the man. In a peremptory tone he said, 'Just make sure my men have a run to Europe if they need it.'

Smiling, Paluzzi began lowering the Marathon Boy back into its case. 'It won't come to that,' he said. 'Frank Paluzzi has a talent for outrunning the police without running at all.'

At a little after 10.30 on Friday night, at the very time Paluzzi joined Serena in her Mini and Robertson tuned in for his first sleep in several days at 'Whiteline', the telephone in the 'Ten of Hearts' club rang and the receptionist who answered heard a terse man's voice ask for Dink. Business in the club had been slack for the evening and Dink was occupying herself before quitting her shift by polishing and cleaning the Sitz baths. When her friend called her to the phone she thought immediately of Abney.

Taking the call on the extension in the massage room, her hackles rose in renewed annoyance when the urbane, cloying voice flowed down the line. Immediately, from the nuance, she knew he'd been boozing – and that something was wrong.

'Dink? How's it going? Everything all right?'

'You bastard,' she said. Her voice was calm. 'You hung up on me last night.'

'Had to. Very busy.' There was a pause of airy, unsteady breathing. 'Listen, I've been doing some work – important work. Me and Gifford – you remember my old chum Giff? I introduced you once.' Dink recalled. Gifford – a small ruthless-looking man with dirty mannerisms, a prison crony. She said nothing. He went on: 'Well, Giff and me stayed together. But we went back to his old Mum's place and Old Bill has a car outside.'

'Old Bill?'

'Yeah, the cops.' Abney coughed, spoke slower. 'Can't see why. Old Giff's cut up. He phoned his Mum and she said they'd been pushin' her. Typical. Victimisation. When anything happens . . . .'

'What have you been at? Where are you?'

The plaintive tone returned. 'Me and Giff came back to Southampton. It's a long story. Look – was anyone looking for me? You know.'

'Tell me what you've been doing? I take it it was more than a chick with hot knickers?'

'I told you. Legit work. Gonna earn a few worthwhile bob out of it. I'll explain later. Now tell me – was anyone round?'

As always with Stan, it was impossible to assess the magnitude of his lying. Was he really with Gifford? Was he in Southampton? Was he really as scared as his voice hinted? Rocking his composure still further might produce more accurate answers. 'Yes,' Dink replied frankly. 'A Superintendent from the Regional Crime Squad called here and at the flat.'

'Bastard. When? Tonight?'

'No, two nights ago.'

Abney's voice tightened. Dink could imagine his gestures of indignation, the gritted teeth, the forehead stretched till every line of frown vanished. 'Why two nights ago? I don't get it. How could they have known? No, it wouldn't make sense. What did he say, for Chrissake?'

'Wanted to speak to you for your own good. Urgently. I intended to tell you last night but . . . .'

Abney seemed choked, nonplussed. 'The shits. Are they tailing you now?'

'I don't think so.' She considered telling him about her suspicions, about the brunette in the Dolomite, but it seemed hysterical somehow. Her tone became fierce again. 'If you've been at it I'm not having anything to do with you. Remember that. Why don't you give the copper a buzz? – I'll give you his number.'

'Balls to the copper. Listen, what would you say to a trip to the States?'

'The States! You're out of your bloody mind. On what? What kind of cash have you got?'

'Nothing yet but it's on its way. I've to meet an American. Big deal in the pipeline. You know me – always after jackpots.'

'I'm not playing along with anything sordid.'

'Look. We can't talk here. Meet me – eh? I'll give you the full story.'

'I'm not going to bloody Southampton.'

'All right. Bond Street on the Central line. Say one tomorrow?'

'You mean the tube?'

The STD pips came and Dink could hear Abney pushing the phone aside and rummaging for change. After a few seconds the line went dead. She slowly replaced the receiver, then gave a shuddering start as she became aware of someone standing behind her. She swivelled and found herself facing Hackett. His face was sanguine, alive. The eyes held her in a kind of flattering closeness that put the fractious chatter of Abney right out of her head. Vaguely she wondered what he had overheard. Did it even matter?

'I've come to be chir-opped,' he smiled.

She looked at her wristwatch. 'At bedtime? I don't believe you. Anyway, this is after-hours for me. I'm supposed to be off at 10.30.'

'Will that cost me more?' The words, she knew, were carefully couched to be teasing, playful. She wasn't sure she wanted to join the game. After all, he was a copper.

She moved back into the body of the massage room and finished her tidying up, pinning up some fresh osteopathic charts and dusting down the Traction machine. Hackett strolled round after her, eyeing the expensive equipment and the wall pictures. He paused at a framed certificate and whistled admiringly. 'Um. Diana Morse MISCh – Member of the Incorporated Society of Chiropodists. Impressive. No wonder I can't get an appointment.' He propped himself on one of the leather-covered trolley tables and watched her take some clothes out of a tie-bag. 'I thought places like this offered more . . . . earthy services.'

Dink excused herself, walked down a side corridor and into a changing cubicle. Over a half-door she spoke to him. 'Are we a disappointment to you?'

'No, I wouldn't say that.' The reply came from close at hand. Dink, absorbed in peeling off her starched white smock, hadn't noticed Hackett move. Now he stood, cool and defiant, leaning over the half-door observing her candid strip. She guessed – rightly – that the strategy was designed to put him at the advantage. But it wouldn't work this time; her body was good, she was proud of it, and it wasn't the first time she had been half-nude in front of a man. When she pulled off the tee shirt that matched the smock her breasts were bare. Keeping her back to Hackett she slipped her bra on, allowed the straps to hang loose, then stepped backwards to the door and applied reverse tactics.

'Do me up, will you?' She watched Hackett's eyes, searching for reaction, but the expression was inscrutably neutral. His hands touched her skin more gently than she had expected, feeling for the flimsy elastic. In a tickly movement the fingers slid under her arms, lightly tracing the swell of each breast, perking them. Then the material was pulled taut and the clip roughly fixed. She waited, but Hackett didn't release her. His hands held her straps tightly and his breath came suddenly down on her shoulder, brushing the skin like warm water. 'Stan been in touch?' he murmured. His lips touched her flesh, then pulled quickly away. All her senses felt alert. She wondered why this copper had really called. His question about Stan somehow seemed of secondary importance to the 'earthy services' one. Was he really only interested in Stan? What was this trouble with Gifford that had Stan worried? What was all this nonsense about the States?

'I haven't heard from him,' she said.

'Oh? Then why did you call me?' The bluff rolled off Hackett's lips sweetly. He could have been a thousand miles out but, receiving the information of a girl's call, he had chosen to be optimistic. Now, confronting her, the brief tinge of redness that suffused her cheek confirmed the assumption.

'Why did you come all the way here? Is it very important, this Stan thing?'

'You'd be doing him and me a favour, luv,' he said. 'I mean it.'

Dink resumed her dressing, pulling her skirt up. 'Well, I wouldn't like to see Stan in trouble – but I'm sure he's enough brains to keep out of it the second time round.'

Indecision fogged her mind. It seemed safer to stick by what Stan wanted. 'But I really can't help you,' she said. 'And – whoever it was – it wasn't me who rang.'

Hackett smiled. 'Do MISCh's tell lies?'

The violet eyes edged away from him. 'Like I said, we're honourable people.' She concluded her dressing, putting on a tight v-neck sweater. 'I presume I'm allowed to go to the ladies' room unaccompanied?' she said.

When she had gone Hackett drifted round the sterile, white massage room. His thoughts were depressed. The girl, he had guessed, was suffering from a beautifully bad case of divided loyalties. Instinct told him she knew more than she was saying but he had expected her to be more forthcoming with gentle goading. Certainly she was the most solid workable link into the hit team, but 'running' her would be harder than he had hoped. Yet still there were peaks of optimism in his mind. The girl didn't want trouble, didn't want Abney in trouble. If he could play that angle, offer some inducement to come clean.

Walking round the room, pacing off his eager thought-train, Hackett distracted himself by perusing the wall charts and discovering, among other things, that legitimate massage, far from being slaps and tickles, encompassed Petrissage, Tapotement, Friction, Kneading and Stroking. Mentally he recited them, conferring them to memory and making a note to recall them to Bonney whose professed interest in massage clubs had him rearing to the prospects of meeting Dink. Hackett had taken sadistic pleasure in spiking his guns, delegating foot-slog work to him instead. Now, Hackett knew, the luckless berk would be drinking tea from a flask, listening to Radio Luxembourg, reading *Deep Throat for Beginners* and indulging himself in similar harmless occupations to while away a night surveillance shift at Gifford's house.

Dink returned, freshly made-up, looking, Hackett

thought, close to beautiful. He said so. Dink laughed and asked chidingly whether Detective Superintendents told lies often. 'How about a drink?' Hackett said. He had visions of getting her pissed, hauling her home, trying the big seduction ploy. Her wry smile mocked his thoughts. 'No,' she said. 'Not that I object to being driven in cop cars but I'm staying overnight with Julie, the manageress. Her guy's away.'

'Another time.'

'Sure.' He walked her through to the reception area where the desk girl – Julie apparently – was closing blinds and switching off lights. Hackett reiterated, asking her to ring if Abney got in touch, but he felt less confident of her now. Loyalties apart, something new had come into play – something that mellowed her feelings towards Abney. Walking to meet Louise in the Capri, he wondered idly if the new factor was money on the horizon.

Louise was dozing in the car, a magazine on her lap. Her scant eye-shadow was smudged, her hair was awry and she looked about a hundred years old. Hackett nudged her awake. He clicked on the UHF and asked one of his cars in London to pick him up. 'Any luck?' Louise asked, blinking into life at last.

'Don't I look happy?' he jibed. 'I've been doing finger exercises on white lace bras.'

'Loaded or unloaded?'

'Judge for yourself.' He nodded forward. 'Here they come – coming round the corner. You know Dink, the smallish blonde?' Louise said yes. 'Right. I want you to follow. Stick close. She's my odds-on favourite. Might almost be worth getting a phone tap on her.' He slipped out of the car.

Seemingly unconcerned about the possibilities of a tail, Dink climbed casually into the girl Julie's car without as much as a glance round. Hackett stood in a doorway and saw the car pull off, turn and drive back in his direction. Louise promptly dived down, out of sight, as the beams of headlights knifed across the street. As the car motored past she resurfaced, waited two minutes, then fired the engine and accelerated off in pursuit.

Lennie, the Squad man doing roving co-ordinator between the surveillance teams around London, picked Hackett up in twenty minutes. Before driving out of London they stopped at an all-night café and discussed the possibilities of Paluzzi already having smuggled the treasures out of the country. Hackett thought it unlikely and checks – even from Heathrow and Eastleigh – had turned up nothing; all traffic seemed legit and no plane or boat had gone unaccounted for.

At midnight the news summary blared over the proprietor's transistor did nothing to quench the Squad men's sombre mood. There were no new developments in inquiries and the security guard injured in the raid had died.

Hackett received the grim report without comment. In a twisted way the death helped him. It gave him more teeth to bite with. Now, for Abney and whoever else was involved in the hit, the stakes had altered drastically. The crime was no longer robbery – it was murder.

6

There were topless girls and spectral steamers bulging with arms floating across the heath. It was night-time but the sun was shining and a bronze statue in the centre of the world occupied every soul's attention. Hackett wasn't interested in the statue. Neither was Paluzzi. Hackett could see him, hiding behind the boat with a Luger in his fist. Hackett was crouched in cover too, but he would have to get closer soon, he would have to take the risk and break cover. Paluzzi, like a wraith in sunlight, was beginning to fade. It was now or never. With a supreme effort of will, his whole body screaming at him to stop, Hackett dashed out of hiding and ran towards Paluzzi. He pulled his gun up. His body was trembling. Paluzzi was aiming his Luger. *Don't shoot*. Hackett was coming nearer. Paluzzi was about to fire. Hackett could see the glisten of oil on the gun and of pomade in his hair. Paluzzi fired. Hackett took the bullet in his head, shouted a last cry of life and buckled on the ground. And then he realised it wasn't him dead at all – it was someone else, a good friend, a good copper . . . .

The telephone shrilled and Hackett was plucked back into reality.

Crawling across the bed on his stomach, his body still weak with tension, he whipped up the receiver.

'Dink's made contact with Abney.' It was Bonney's voice, hoarse, charged with success. For a long moment Hackett wasn't sure his dream had ended. Across the room his own image glared back at him from the mirror: the tousled, scowling entity looked rough enough to be real.

'Where? Are you covering it?'

'Café in Oxford Street. I joined Louise. We did a double-up when shifts changed at two. Alternated kips in the back, you know.'

'Right. How long is it on?'

'She took a tube from her friend's pad in Clapham. Went from Tottenham Court Road round to Bond Street. They joined up there. No more than twenty minutes. What'll I do?'

'Don't lose him. I'll come up.'

'Who else'll I inform?'

'Leave it to me. Now tell me where you are.'

A minute later Hackett rang off and began dressing hurriedly. Breakfast could wait, everything else could wait. If this was on, if this *was* Abney, the whole deal was as good as in his pocket. But he would have to play it cautiously.

'You sure you won't have something to eat?' Abney piled his plate high with the chips Dink had abandoned. Aside from the drawn, anxious look on his face, Dink saw, the only other thing that was untypically Stan was the disconcerting habit he had suddenly acquired of constantly examining people around. From the moment they met in the underground, she knew he was in big trouble.

'I'm not hungry.' Her voice dropped to an urgent whisper, though the nearest other customers in the café were three tables away. 'What's all this secrecy? That copper called again. I want to know what you've been doing.'

'Can't you guess?'

'Don't look so bloody smug. C'mon. Tell me. Another job with Gifford?'

With childish glee, through a mouthful of food, Abney

beamed at her. 'You see the telly – The Marathon Boy, those Greek peaches? The brilliant hit?'

Dink fell back limp in her chair. A teaspoon slipped from her hand and clattered noisily onto the formica table top. 'Jesus, you don't mean . . . *you*!'

Abney's cheery smile died. He gripped her hand across the table. His teeth barred briefly and the fingertips pinched her wrist. 'Hey, play it easy,' he hissed. 'I'm risking my neck as it is coming along here. You sure you weren't followed? What did the cop say when he came back?'

'I'm pretty certain I wasn't followed. I was on the look-out.' Dink was having difficulty controlling her face. The Greek treasure, for God's sake. Every bloody paper had it as headline news. If they caught him for this he'd be an old man before he'd see the light of day again. And then that guard had died.

Her body grew rigid and her hands started trembling. 'They suspect you,' she said shakily. 'Hackett – '

Abney smiled wanly. 'Ah, Robertson's friend. We expected him.'

'He wanted to know about you and some friend called . . . Pallaby or – '

'Paluzzi.' Abney's voice was distant, stunned. He had stopped eating and stared at Dink, his thoughts racing. 'How could Hackett have known about Paluzzi? *That's* what must have started him. I'll bet Paluzzi cocked up his end of it, silly bloody shit!'

'But they'll crucify you for this, Stan. This isn't ten per cent of two wankers. That stuff is priceless.'

A short twinkle of pride lit Abney's face. The bastard was too thick to understand how big a stir he was causing. Dink leant forward to speak with emphasis. 'If I was you I'd cut losses and get the hell out of this country – now.'

'That's exactly what I want to do. What I'm going to do. And you'll come with me.'

'Be sensible. You've nothing – '

'Tomorrow I'll have seventy grand.'

'How? Ransom?' It was an effort even to speak the words.

'Too roundabout for me. No I'm selling the gear. Sweeter and cleaner. All I've to do is get it to Ireland. Quick run, no problems. Then I'm taking the cash and heading for the States or Mexico City.'

What about Gifford – and I presume there were others?'

'Too bad for them. Paluzzi can pay them expenses. He's a generous tinker.'

'You mean . . . . you're going to double-cross? The others don't know you're going to sell?'

'Paluzzi is a mean shit – genuinely. As far as I'm concerned he's using us, the team. When it's all over he'll dump us. We're too dicey for a bum like that. He wants a clean front in Britain, and we'd be a deadweight. He'll probably get his Mafia chums to push us out. Christ knows where we'd end up. Now I know he's got the stuff in this cover warehouse, y'see. All I've to do is get myself a lorry and a driver – something authentic, solid, working the London-Dublin run maybe. Then I slip the Bronze Boy in with the gear. Remember I told you, we did that once long time ago, shiftin' stolen TV's?'

'It's crazy.'

'It's bloody wise, girl. Especially if the squad has wind of the team. Old Giff'll crack. He was never right for this job. I'm clearing out while the going's good. And you can come along for the ride.'

'And what about the . . . . team? Where are they now – in hiding?'

'Working out alibis. Like me. 'Cept I maybe should have filled you in in the beginning, eh? But Robertson – he's the organiser – he wanted us quick. There was a lot of planning necessary. But it went like a dream. See what the *Mail* said?'

'They'll come after you and kill you. And the cops'll never let go.'

'*Greek* stuff? 'Course they will. It's not Her Majesty's mail this time. In six months I'll be sunning it in Mexico and the whole performance'll be painful memory. 'Cept for me.' Abney's hands reached over and cupped Dink's. His face assumed a curious pathos that was both beguiling and alarming. He *wanted* this one. He wanted to win. When he looked at her this way Dink found it hard to refuse him. 'Sticking round is the danger,' he said gravely. 'The squad obviously want Paluzzi – he's ex-Mafia, y'see. Their fight's with him. So it makes sense every way to scarper. Don't you see that?' His eyes became pleading. 'Well, what about it, baby? Will you come along? Seventy to play with. I could buy a little shop.'

Dink laughed shortly. 'Oh come on. You wouldn't work an honest day if the Queen herself begged you.' Abney drew her hands closer. 'Come on,' he said. 'It's my swan song. I want to make it work. And I want you in.'

For a throbbing moment Dink said nothing. Then, with a clear-voiced enthusiasm she wasn't feeling she said, 'How would we get out of the country?'

With a laugh of relief and victory Abney began telling her.

Across the road from the café Louise left the walk-around shoe shop from where she had been keeping the entrance under view, and sauntered to the magazine shop where Bonney was catching up with his *Punch* reading. She sidled up to Bonney and looped her arm through his in an intimate husband-and-wife fashion. Her eyes drifted up from his magazine. Ahead, through the display window, there was an unobstructed view over to the café. 'He's bound to move soon,' she whispered. Bonney shuffled irritably. 'Hackett won't be long. It's an hour now. Anyway, he's well covered. Gavin's parked down behind the C & A opposite Marble Arch and Chick's up at Charing Cross.' He moved position as a knot of shoppers in the street blocked the line of vision. 'Problem is the location. All these people. Abney's no fool.'

For fifteen more minutes Louise and Bonney lingered, browsing. Then they walked out into Oxford Street and meandered through a succession of walk-in clothes shops. By mutual agreement Louise went back to their car, parked a minute's walk away, to check on Hackett's progress. Just then, as Bonney moved into an ice cream parlour, Abney emerged from the café. Bonney veered off, ran across the road through lanes of immobile buses and took position several hundred yards away behind Abney. There was no sign of Dink, but that wouldn't matter. Bonney stuck close to Abney because of the swirling eddies of pedestrians, surging around, ambling at wide angles across the pavements, slowing people down. Luckily, blessedly, he was heading in the direction of Louise. Bonney pulled up. Abney had stopped and was glancing back up the street, looking for a bus perhaps, or a taxi to take him westwards. A minute passed – and, sure enough, Abney stepped off the pavement and flagged down a black cab. Bonney started running. Traffic was heavy and the cab wouldn't advance far. He quickly outpaced it and ran into the side street where Louise was sitting apparently filing her nails in the Dolomite. She immediately guessed what had happened. Before Bonney had pulled the door shut she had the engine roaring and was edging into traffic. 'He's headed for Marble Arch. There's no entry for private cars into Oxford Street but we'll try it. Go.'

With little trouble, before Marble Arch, they located the taxi. Bonney tried to raise Gavin on the UHF but failed. He turned to Louise and asked about Hackett. 'He's in. Stuck in congestion coming up New King's Road.' Bonney started to call Hackett. A tinny whine whistled out of the receiver and Bonney's voice rebounded back to him, echoing loud. He slapped the panel in which the UHF was housed. 'Christ, we're not going to be cut out, are we? Radio's off.' A statical rattling started, hollow yet grating, like the deafening silence of putting one's ear against a whorl shell. It set Louise's teeth on edge. Bonney twisted the volume down and suddenly, briefly, Hackett's call came over. 'Going north. Old Brompton. D'you read?' Bonney jabbed the transmit switch. 'Affirmative. Radio problem. Following taxi. Notting Hill Gate, west. Follow D'you read, Hackett?' The static really began then. A flash of Hackett's voice came over, requesting exact position. Bonney shouted over, 'Now at Holland Park Tube, headed west' – He read off the taxi reg. When he had finished talking and released the switch the scream of the radio made him turn off immediately. Louise sighed. 'Better not lose our friend. Traffic lights are a problem here.'

'Stick up close. Take no chances,' Bonney ordered. Louise darted forward, overtook too hastily and got herself stuck in the outside slower lane entering a roundabout. Momentarily the traffic in her lane came to a full stop and the taxi slid along on the inside, a good distance away, and moved out of view. Bonney cursed savagely. He jerked up the UHF again and started wildly calling Hackett. The radio was totally dead, buzzing quietly now. Louise, infuriated by her miscalculation, took the first gap in the inner lanes, sped in, accelerated fast, expertly dodged a heavy-vehicle snarl-up, crossed lanes a half-dozen times and soared into the roundabout. 'Where do we go now?' Bonney snapped. 'No sign of the taxi. We'll have to chance it. Pull hard left.' Louise obeyed, turning tightly and moving fast down a wide, almost empty road. Repeatedly Bonney tried to call Hackett, but with no success. They were heading, Louise knew, for Kensington. Not, she recalled from Abney's file, native country. She wondered were they on line. And then Bonney shouted out. Ahead. The taxi was ahead. They had guessed right.

Well familiar with the techniques of good follows, Louise brought the car up close to the taxi, then casually allowed it to dawdle as other traffic overtook and cut in. At Kensington High Street the taxi turned left and motored back towards the West End. Bonney slumped back in his seat for a second. 'That ain't right,' he murmured. 'This is going in a circle. Get back up there – quick.' Risking the wrath of crazy city drivers, Louise angled out and started weaving through the bus and slow lanes, taking advantage of the smaller flow of cars.

On Bonney's order she drew right alongside the taxi as it slowed at lights, coming near Knightsbridge. They both craned tensely forward, stared into the taxi's rear compartment. A constricting pain of disappointment and self-annoyance gripped Bonney's chest. Louise, uncharacteristically, spat an oath. The taxi carried no passenger. Somewhere along the line, while they were stalled in the traffic jam, Abney had been let out.

'Stop the cab,' Bonney told Louise, his voice truculent. 'We've blown it.'

Rain started early on Saturday night – a hard, very wet rain that kept the drifters, tourists and hookers off the streets and kept the pub-crawlers anchored to one bar. Dink had met her friend Julie in a Clapham pub where they had had a meal and sat over a few too many drinks while waiting for the downpour to retreat. Finally, with no sign of capitulation from the elements, Dink had insisted on making a start for home. Julie objected, asking Dink to stay at her place another night despite the fact that her partner was home, but Dink was adamant: she wanted to get away, wanted to be by herself and think, *decide*. At nine, leaving Julie amongst a lively group, she headed off, taking a bus and walking the rest of the way, stubbornly braving the chill of drizzle.

The soaking rain half-sobered her and she entered her flat feeling considerably fresher than she'd been since lunchtime, with just a mild headache ruffling her mood. The velvety darkness of the room, like a welcome ablution, eased her pain immediately and she left the light off, crossed to the venetian blinds of the living-room, closed them and flopped into a deep-chair. After a minute, uneasy with the ghosts that inhabited the room, she stood up and turned on the television. A familiar face washed across the screen – Hayley Mills, pert and snub-nosed and lovely in an old movie. Someone sometime long ago had said she looked just like Hayley Mills. Inwardly she laughed at the memory. It was difficult to believe that once, not too long ago, life was measured in compliments, kisses and broken dates. Now the balance had changed entirely. There was so much more to play for, so much more to gain.

A sudden movement flickered in the shadows and Dink geared forward, her scalp tingling with fright, her headache exploding. As she fumbled to get out of the chair a floor-board creaked and a high protracted sigh sounded. Almost before the light clicked on she knew it was Hackett.

'You told me lies,' he said quietly. Dink shaded her eyes from the glare of light, tried to focus. His posture and the stiff set of his mouth said he knew everything. Dink felt weak, her heart slamming agonisingly in her breast. She opened her mouth but couldn't speak. She tripped back into the chair.

Hackett strolled forward. He knew it was time to turn the screws, play her tough; but for all that he was nervous, scared of forcing too much and losing ground already gained. 'Stan's been in touch. Bond Street tube. The café.

You never told me.'

'You followed me.' Spoken stolidly, it sounded like a declaration of physical violation.

'If you look out your window now you'll see a blue Dolomite. That's one of a fleet. That'll be there all night and it'll be there when you wake up in the morning. That's the way it goes when you join the game.' Hackett sat opposite her, at the edge of a coffee table. He looked callous, she thought, and cynical. Suddenly it was easy to realise why Stan hated these men. People like Hackett took vicious pleasure in degrading, cutting you down. And yet there was an irony in that. These were the men you called when trouble started at the club, or when your car was vandalised, or your bag snatched.

'Did you . . . . did you speak to Stan then?'

Hackett lied smoothly. 'No. We followed him, and we let him think he's stock free. But we didn't pull him in.'

'He didn't do anything.' The words, Dink knew, were hollow. That part of the charade was over.

Ignoring her comment, Hackett talked on. 'Stan's in bad straits, Dink. We have a fair picture of what happened – that Greek stuff – ' He watched her reaction carefully and saw what he wanted. 'We know the people who were involved, Stan's old mates. Apart from the value of the gear they got, a man was killed in the raid. That puts a murder charge over Stan's head. He'll never shake that off. It's twenty years at least for him now. He'll be near seventy before he gets out, he'll be a broken old man.'

Dink's veneer of calm was crumbling. Her fingers toyed with a tissue, shredding it agitatedly. Her eyes were strained, narrow and fast-moving. 'What proof have you got that it was him?'

'Evidence of the security guards,' Hackett lied. 'No two ways about it. Stan'll sink on this one.'

Gathering herself, breathing evenly, Dink said, 'Then it's

all over, is it?'

Hackett spoke fast. 'You know where he's staying?' He desperately wanted the answer to that. A gilded opportunity had been cocked up today by himself and the squad. They had Abney and they lost him. Hackett shouldn't have played it so close to the chest. He should have drafted more Yard men in, should have pulled Abney while the going was good. Instead the follow misfired and they ended up with nothing. Nothing except Dink.

'I don't know where he is,' she said sharply. 'But presumably you do.'

Hackett evaded that. 'But I want more than Stan, Dink. I want the top men, the planners. And I want the gear.' When she said nothing he pushed on, his tone softening. 'That's where Stan could do himself a favour.'

'I don't understand.' Her eyes were diverted, blankly staring at the TV.

'How much has he told you? Do you know where the goods are?'

'Of course not. Stan's only one of the fellas. The ringleader has 'em.'

'Paluzzi?' The word broke up in Hackett's mouth, the syllables coming separately.

Dink nodded silently. Hackett balled a fist and sank it gently into an open palm. He resisted the temptation to shout his victory. *Paluzzi!* Confirmation. Proof. The bastard was at it, digging his own grave.

'Look,' Hackett goaded. 'Only one thing'll make it easier for Stan and that's the return of this gear and a clean wrap-up for us.'

'Stan won't grass.'

'I know. Lessons learnt last time. But you can do the favour for him.'

'How?'

'Get me onto Paluzzi, get details for me. In return I'll

guarantee you a sympathetic hearing for Stan.'

'That means nothing. I've read about that sort of pressure.'

'I'm as good as my word, luv. I'm being good to Stan. And you. I could pull Stan in now – and you – and give you purgatory.' He paused, repeated with emphasis, 'But I want Paluzzi.'

Calm again, Dink got up and paced the room. Her eyes still avoided Hackett's. 'I know a lot about Stan,' she said. 'And he told me, he didn't kill that guard. He hadn't got a stick. The man, he said, was hit.'

'Good,' Hackett said. 'That'll help him. If you can get more facts for me I can build up a picture that'll help Stan. After all, luv, those berks aren't going to stick their necks out to look after him. They're hard bastards.'

Dink had come to a stop at the window, her back to Hackett. Already she knew what she wanted to do and the speed of her decision surprised her a little. When she gave it a minute's thought it came clear in her mind. Hackett's ultimatum was a relief to her because it cancelled out the options; Stan's double-cross plan was dead; there were no real decisions of loyalty left to be made. Either way, Hackett had him. She turned to face him.

'I could try and persuade Stan to come in.'

'So could I,' Hackett smiled. 'But you know the code. He won't spill. I want the others. Paluzzi.'

'I don't know if I could help.' Dink said. 'Not with Paluzzi. But I might be able to help you to the gear. You see – ' She gulped in air. 'Stan wants to take if off Paluzzi, to try to sell it himself. He's set up a deal with an American and he's just got to move the stuff to Ireland.'

'Have you any idea where the stuff is? I presume Paluzzi wants to ransom it?'

Dink nodded. 'It's in a warehouse somewhere. That's all I know. Stan wants to fix up with a lorry to shift it – in with groupage, mixed cargo or something, you know.'

'When?'

'I dunno. He had to finalise details with the American, but he's hoping for tomorrow maybe. I suppose a lot depends on the driver he's looking for.' She frowned in concentration. 'If you're following him, you could watch his contacts and follow them on – couldn't you? That way you'd get the driver.'

Mindful of the risk of rushing in too early on Abney and alerting Paluzzi, another more positive idea came to Hackett. There would be dangers but, if it worked, it would limit the possibilities of blowing out, and forge a definite link *into* the team. 'When will you be seeing Stan again?' he said.

'I won't. He didn't like the notion of me having his address, in case you came knocking.' She smiled slightly. 'But he'll be ringing tonight – to tell me if tomorrow's on.'

'Trustful bastard, isn't he?' Dink pulled a face. He went on, 'You could give my boys an in. Tell Stan you know a driver who'll take the gear.'

Her violet eyes opened wide and her jaw dropped. 'You're joking,' she stammered. 'He'd never believe me.'

'Why not? He's not that well in with your mates from the club, is he? Tell him it's a friend of Julie's. Someone he doesn't know.'

Dink stared hard at Hackett. 'You know what you're asking me to do?' she said dully. 'Cheat on him, double-cross – walk him into a police net.'

'It'll be worth it. I'll stick up for him when it comes to court. Say he helped out. He'll get off lightest. I promise that.'

Dink's unwavering look was vaguely disconcerting. She'd been around long enough, Hackett mused, to know just how much men would pledge, swear, lie, to get what they badly wanted. Tomorrow morning the promises would be forgotten.

'Stan would kill me if he found out. And the rest of the gang – I mean, I don't know what they'd do.'

'I'll be right behind you.'

'No you won't.' Her voice was brittle now. The cheeks looked hot. 'You can send that bloody chick in the Dolomite round all right, but who holds my hand when I'm in bed, when I'm at work, when I'm here by myself? If something goes wrong, if the gang found out, or Stan – ' She stopped abruptly, her words pitched loud. Hackett stood up and took her by the arms. Instinctively she tore away, the heat of tears burning her eyes. Christ, it was ridiculous! She was feeling sorry for herself, cursing Stan for messing up a good thing they had going; for coming close to earning a lot of bread, then throwing it away; for ever entering into fight with a fella like Hackett.

Hackett touched her cheek, held her firmly round the waist with one hand. 'Here, now,' he said quietly. 'You don't think I'd let you get into trouble, do you? I'm only asking you 'cause you're my only way in. If I don't do it this way, all I've got is the option of homing in on Stan, pulling him and nailing him. You're giving him an advantage, luv. But that's between you and me. No one need know. Stan won't even know, if that's what you want.'

'He might have a driver already.' The words were choked with tears.

'Chance we'll take. But if he doesn't . . . ' Her body had relaxed now and lay against his, yielding and soft. There were bubbles of rain still on her cheeks and the smooth skin in the neckline of her dress shimmered under a film of dampness. Her head was tilted down, and Hackett could see that the eyelashes were wet too. He pulled her chin up. The eyes had surrendered too. Hackett said, 'Even if Stan got away with his plan, even if he swindled the gear from Paluzzi, he'd never live to enjoy it. Paluzzi isn't that sort of cowboy. He's a deadly bugger. He'd get after Stan. There'd be no let up. My fight – ' He paused, realising he was saying far more than he had to, ' – is with Paluzzi. I know the man. I want him in 'cause he's a murderer and a stirrer. Five years ago he tried to start up here, came down south, began a business to cover for running arms to Northern Ireland. I was a Squad Inspector at the time. The Super in charge of operations – the guy I succeeded – worked hard at building a case against Paluzzi. Finally we got info that he was preparing to take arms in. We set up a counter-move to arrest him and take the arms. The thing was a total cock-up.' Hackett's eyes drifted over Dink's head, remembering. 'Paluzzi changed tactics at the last minute and we had to run after him, rush a few men down to a different wharf. We were outnumbered and when we tried to take him all hell broke loose. I've never seen a rat fight so viciously to get out of a trap. Paluzzi shot three men, three good mates of mine. Two of 'em pulled through but the third died. He was the Super, the top man. Paluzzi cut him down and the guy wasn't even armed. That's the kind of bastard he is. Life and death mean nothing to him.' Dink, Hackett saw suddenly, was staring up at him with non-comprehending eyes. The facts he was relating were too far removed from prostitution and tax dodging and Stan's petty pilfering to be believable. What would a man like Stan have in common with a killer like Paluzzi? Was it even the same game?

Hackett said, 'Stan has nothing to gain in this trick of his. With Paluzzi involved he loses every way.'

'Then so do I,' she replied. Before she had finished speaking, before she could protest further, Hackett's mouth pressed down on her lips. At first she didn't respond, then her legs shifted closer, the firm thighs caressing his, the warm swell of her belly crushing into his hips. They broke away.

'That sets the seal on our agreement,' Hackett grinned, grateful for the spontaneity.

In a more friendly voice she said, 'Would you like that drink now? If you have the time, I have . . .'

Hackett flopped down into her chair. 'Sure I've time,' he said. 'Even for a bit of Petrissage, Tapotement, Friction, Kneading and Stroking.' He watched her beautiful legs as she strode off to fetch a drinks tray but his thoughts were fixed on Abney. It would be a good idea to linger, to be here when the call came through. When she came back into the room he focussed on her less distractedly. The blue cotton dress moulded her curves lovingly, lending accent to the long narrow waist and the generous hips. Abney slipped from his mind. It would be a good idea to linger anyway.

Near eleven the telephone started ringing.

Mixing ingredients for a curry supper in the kitchen, Dink abandoned tools and walked quickly out to answer it. Hackett sauntered after her, observing the tension that stiffened her face and voice. The caller was Abney and he hadn't yet found his driver. In a halting voice Dink started telling him about her friend's friend.

When she hung up she looked over to Hackett, wide-eyed and shaking. 'It's OK,' she said. 'He believed me. He wants me to bring the guy into town to meet him.'

'Good girl,' Hackett said. He kissed her on the forehead.

7

'You made a balls of it somewhere. Even before we started the crime squad was on to us. A copper called Hackett was prowlin' around, looking for you.'

Even though it was full daytime, with a high sun and pleasant warmth in the air, the blinds in the flat over 'The Golden Gun' club were drawn tight and crepuscular darkness clouded the room. Paluzzi sat smoking, coolly watching Gifford, in mac and hat, swaying heatedly in the middle of the floor. Already, in ten minutes, he had told Gifford three times to tone his voice down, that people might overhear, but Gifford wasn't in a reasoning mood. Paluzzi contained his annoyance by biting the tip of his tongue. At length he cut in on Gifford's rambling.

'You've broken the rules, Gifford,' he said. 'Firstly, I told you all to keep apart. Robertson tells me you teamed up with Abney. That was fool-hardy. My intention for you all was to create sound covers, with nothing linking you. Obviously you felt you could do better by yourself. You should at least have told Robertson.' He paused to inhale his cheroot but the manacing stare stopped Gifford from speaking. 'And now you come here in a state of excitement, shouting the place down. You should not have come here. Who told you I was here?'

'That doesn't matter,' Gifford barked, unwilling to implicate Robertson who had trustingly given them all a good picture of the Italian they were working for. 'What matters is the game's blown. Abney told me. You shouldn't have started it with the squad sniffing round. And Abney says you'd trouble with that squad before. Couple of years back over smuggling. Hackett has it in for you.'

'Has he now?' Paluzzi's voice had grown louder. The little man was disgusting. Not only was he unprofessional and apparently nervy, but he stank to high heaven. Unthinkingly Paluzzi held his cheroot under his nostrils and sniffed the curling smoke to kill the smell. 'But, don't you see, Gifford, none of this matters provided I can get the ransom cash and you get your share. And I've no reason to doubt that won't happen. Everything is going very well and – '

'*Well!* You're bleedin' joking, mate. My mother's being hounded by the squad. There's a twenty-four-hour watch on the house. She can't go out but there's a son-of-a-bastard trailin' on. As soon as any of us show our clocks we're screwed. Hackett's a pig's crutch, y'know. He has a reputation.'

'Very interesting I'm sure. But, if that's the case, Robertson will arrange passages to Europe. That was my original concept and the one he – and you all – liked. That was the basis of our agreement.'

'But you shouldn't have started – '

Paluzzi stood up brusquely and crossed to Gifford. In his characteristic way he stood squarely in front of him and stared levelly. It was a trick he'd learnt from a pickpocket in Naples during the war; stand close to a person, engage all their attention with your eyes, talk with emphasis and deliberation. Done cleverly you could absorb them enough to easily rifle their pockets – the pickpocket called it 'the snake look'. 'Does Abney know you've come here?' Gifford shook his head roughly. Paluzzi went on. 'In twenty-four hours I expect the ransom will have been paid. Then we can start moving you out.'

'I'm not waiting twenty-four hours, mate. I want out now.'

'It's impossible,' Paluzzi sighed. 'My friends will have to be told, time will be needed.'

'Bugger your dago friends. I'll look after myself. I want cash now. I'll settle for less than starting price. Fifteen grand.'

'I don't have fifteen,' Paluzzi smiled amiably. 'If I had good cash I wouldn't have come all the way here to set up, would I? But tomorrow – '

'I'm not waiting round. If the squad have you in sight now, what'll it be after the pull? I'll take ten, eight – '

Paluzzi forced a small laugh. He spoke as equably as possible. 'I feel sure you'll be happy if you wait till tomorrow. How many times in the past has rash action caused problems? It's always better to be calm.'

'You don't have ten bloody years in the box behind you, do you? If I go in now I'll never see fish 'n chips again, mate. No. I've given you your go, you've cocked-up a job. I should've turned Robertson down when he came to see me. There's too much noise round this caper. I should've known.'

'Yes, maybe you should have.'

Gifford moved away from Paluzzi, but his eyes stayed fixed, brutal and challenging now. The Italian, he thought, looked downcast, defeated. Gifford was glad he came, proud of his independence. He'd told Robertson on the phone. If Paluzzi didn't do something, didn't pay him off now before trouble really started, he'd go straight to him. He knew the name of the club and he had a fair idea of its location. It would only take him a few hours to search it down. He wasn't afraid of meddling dagos who thought they could fake a passport and make a bloody fortune at the Englishman's expense. Like he told Robertson, he should never have joined this one, the whole job was a bummer – a repeat of the kidnap fiasco that had cost them all so dearly. Paluzzi carried the Mafia curse with him, he was bad luck. 'I wasn't gonna take this job at all, you know,' he said unnecessarily, his voice raised to a near-shout. 'Only Robertson was in this town and heard I was here.'

The door opened and Serena walked in, dressed casually in jeans and a blousy sweater. She glanced suspiciously to Gifford, frowning her disapproval. 'We have people from the gaming club in checking the tables downstairs, Frank. The noise – '

Paluzzi waved her angrily away. The door closed. Gifford snickered. 'Nice bit of tit. It's a miserable game this, isn't it? There's always winners like you and poor buggers like me.'

Paluzzi said, 'I think you'd better go now. Tomorrow I'll arrange a meeting with Robertson. Then, when the ransom is in we'll fix up what goes.'

'Abney says you're onto a bummer and I believe him. I want something now.'

'I have nothing to give you.'

'Well I have you, mate. I know this place, don't I? That's enough. 'Tits' downstairs'll fill in the picture for the coppers.'

'Are you threatening me, Gifford?'

'I'm saying as I *could* threaten you – see?'

Paluzzi closed his eyes and ran his hands gently over his slicked-back hair. His expression looked infinitely serene. When he opened his eyes again he was smiling. 'Three grand?' he said.

Gifford's eyes lit up. He had the bastard! But three grand was an insult. He shook his head. 'Too little. Eight.'

'One moment then.' Paluzzi turned and walked behind the settee. He reached up and slowly pulled the curtain that divided the room across. Gifford could not now see him. But he heard him. A drawer in the dressing-table creaked open and there was a sound of rustling paper.

Paluzzi coughed. Then a match was struck and billows of tobacco smoke glided over the curtain-top. Gifford knew he would have to be careful of cheating here. Paluzzi might pack the cash into something and stuff paper in with it; or he might mix hundred bills with tenners.

Whistling casually, Gifford moved up to the curtain. There was one chink in the rosebud brocade where two strips of material were tied into one curtain. Placing himself beside this he looked in. Paluzzi's back was to him, but he could see the insipid blues and greens of money on the dresser. Paluzzi seemed to be counting it out of the drawer, but it was difficult to see. 'I hear you're intending to launder the ransom cash through a company in the Isle of Man,' Gifford said conversationally. 'That must be a piece of cake. I suppose you just purchase capital stock and realise it in time? Wish I had that kind of business head. But then, the Mafia are known for that kind of thing, aren't they?'

'Who told you about the Isle of Man? Robertson?'

Gifford laughed. 'Now, I shouldn't say, should I? But, yes, he told me. Trying to impress me with how 'perfect' everything was. Holds you in high regard, does Robertson.'

'One does one's best. I've always tried to be a thorough worker. And the Bronze Boy job is as near perfect as any – no matter what you say about this Hackett.' Paluzzi leant back and touched the curtain with his heel. 'Come here, will you?' Gifford pulled the curtain aside and strolled in. His eyes lit on the cash spread on the dresser amid Balmain and wine bottles. There was a lot there, but not enough – not eight grand, not even three. Gifford went to open his mouth but Paluzzi interjected. 'Here,' he said, 'Hold my cigar, eh?' Gifford took the half-burnt cheroot. As he did, in an easy fluid movement Paluzzi grabbed his wrist and jerked him inwards, towards his chest. Off balance, Gifford tried to fall aside, out of the grip, but

Paluzzi had tremendous strength in his hands. Gifford crashed into him with such force that he bounced away rapidly, breaking Paluzzi's hold. As he steadied himself he suddenly felt a smarting sensation in his side. He looked down and a swift wave of weakness passed over him. There was blood on his mac – Paluzzi had cut him. He glanced across to Paluzzi. His vision swam. Paluzzi's eyes were narrow and crazed. The teeth, cheap plastic and yellowed, were visible, clenched tight. There was something shining in the hand – Gifford caught a short glimpse of it before Paluzzi lunged forward, throwing the right hand out. Gifford side-stepped but didn't move fast enough. A searing pain that exploded in his stomach and shot through his entire body riveted him. Now Paluzzi was getting ready to strike again and he could not defend himself. The object in his hand shone brightly now and Gifford saw it plainly – a long-blade bread knife with serrations on one edge. Used, as Paluzzi was working it, in a sawing motion, it made a barbarous weapon. Dragging up every ounce of strength, Gifford slumped left of Paluzzi as the knife thrust out. A ripping noise sounded as the blade sank through the light cloth of the mac. Gifford remembered the cheroot in his fingers. He whipped his hand up and rammed the burning end into Paluzzi's eyes. Paluzzi let out a muted scream, covering his eyes with his left hand and plunging savagely with the knife. Gifford tried to run but the knife was too fast. As he twisted away the blade buried itself deep in his back, carving in over the kidneys and pulling hard down. Gifford opened his mouth to scream and Paluzzi saw the gesture. Forcing the knife in further, he drew up his other hand and pushed the fingers down Gifford's throat. The scream diminished to a rattling croak. Blood surged up the throat and dribbled out of the mouth. Paluzzi held the dying body fast, pulling it greedily to him as one might hold a child's body. The knife was in as far as it would go.

The eyes had become misty and opaque. Paluzzi watched the eyes anxiously. In half-a-minute he saw what he wanted, what he had seen so many times before. Life, like a shadow of nothing, skipped from the wide pupils and Gifford relaxed into deadweight in his arms. Gently, cautiously, he tore down one of the strips of curtain with his free hand, while keeping the body upright with the other. Then he lay Gifford onto the heavy material and began wrapping up the corpse. He had folded the material just once when the door opened and Serena rushed in looking panicky.

'The noise,' she muttered. 'Downstairs, I heard a shout –'

She stood stock still when she saw the twisted limbs on the floor. Paluzzi's hands were blood-stained and his clothing was dishevelled. 'It's all right,' he said. 'The man attacked me. I had to defend myself.' Serena saw his eyes were marked, blackened, one eye was closed, burnt. Stupidly she mumbled, 'Are you all right?' He nodded. 'But he's dead. I had to. Help me.'

Serena took a few paces forward then drew to a stop. The air was full of appalling smells – the odour of the man's body, the smell of sweat and of raw meat. Blood was seeping through the brocade material, turning the rosebuds purple. Her mouth was parched and when she swallowed bile trickled up. 'I . . . I can't,' she said. 'Jesus, Frank, what can you do with . . . with that?'

'No problem,' Paluzzi snapped. His voice was fierce. 'Quick,' he shouted. 'Get me tissue, toilet paper to soak up the blood. And a wet towel for my eyes . . .'

Gripped in a violent paroxysm of shaking, Serena ran to the connecting bathroom. Throwing a large towel into the sink she ran water on it till it was wet through. Then, pulling as much tissue as she could from spare toilet rolls, she rushed back into the living-room. She handed it all to Paluzzi and retreated, aghast.

Except for the tension in his voice, she perceived,

Paluzzi was totally calm. It struck her suddenly that this man was of an alien spieces that no ordinary person could identify with. Fascinated by money and the lure of a 'name', Serena had surrendered her virginity and her soul to him six years ago. She had been, she knew, just one of a long line of pretty women he leeched upon – women who, knowingly or otherwise, supplied him with a respectable facade and whom he often cunningly manipulated as devices in his criminal plots. But Serena had given in blindly to him. She had been twenty-five, a retiring but self-possessed girl who knew she was too good-looking, too bright, for the limbo of working class marriage in Milan. She had wanted to better herself socially and Paluzzi had come along driving a flash car and glittering like a burnished gem. He had given her money if not style, and in return she gave him her body and a dogged loyalty he expected from women. For a year she worked with him but he had jealously guarded her from the outward aspects of his business: she might smuggle something across a border for him, but if she did she would never be aware of its value, or whether it was stolen, or what he had planned for it; if she were caught she might claim convincingly that she knew nothing at all about the contraband, that it had been planted on her. This vacuum that Paluzzi kept her in did not insulate her against 'rumours' that came through about her lover's trade. She had heard stories of his brutality, of the callousness with which he killed unfaithful servants, but she had never spoken to him about this kind of thing and had certainly never witnessed anything. To her, overtly he had always been a gentle man with a keen mind whose involvement in shady businesses satisfied a kink in an otherwise balanced personality. Because of the gentleness of his everyday manners, and his kindness in bed, Serena had found it inconceivable to think of him as a cold-blooded killer. And yet, because of the rumours, she had always suspected.

And now she was seeing with her own eyes.

She wasn't certain why this dirty little man had died, but she had observed the seething rage with which Paluzzi had greeted him and it had unnerved her. She had guessed there would be trouble, but hadn't expected this. She thought of her position with the club. The owner might never find out, because he was a retired man, an invalid who rarely visited the place and never came upstairs; but the other staff would be bothersome. Some of the stewards regularly came up for a drink and her girl friends often stayed the night. She said this to Paluzzi and he shrugged. 'A little blood spot here and there on the carpet.' he said. 'That's all. Some detergent will clear it up.' He was unwinding the body. Now he pinched the knife out of the torso and tossed it onto a pad of tissue. Methodically he began covering the bloodied areas with thick tissue wads and rolling the curtain up again. When he had finished he hefted the body up and threw it onto the settee. Serena cried out. 'For God's sake, Frank. You're not going to just leave it, are you?'

Paluzzi took her firmly by the wrists. His right eye was closed, scorched, but the left was unmarked. In a demanding voice he said, 'There will be no connection between this man and here. I will see to that. You know I don't take chances. This is unfortunate, but it's all right. What happened was unavoidable. The man wanted to compromise me.'

He waited, holding Serena tightly, until her face relaxed and her breathing regulated itself. Then he sat in an armchair and lit a cheroot. Serena, transfixed, stood staring at the body. 'I've made mistakes,' Paluzzi said evenly. 'I should not have entered into business with old friends. There are too many links to me. If that man can find me the police can find me.' He met Serena's eyes as they turned, frightened, to him. He smiled. 'I said to you a short time ago, this club doesn't suit you. I think the time has come for both of us to move on.'

'Was he – ' Serena nodded to the trussed up body, ' – one of the team that hit the Greek stuff?'

'There's no point in keeping any more from you, is there? Yes, he is one of them. But that won't affect the business. It is up to me alone to finalise the deal.'

'Then I was right. It's ransom, isn't it? You have the stuff in Newbury and you're organising the ransom. That's why you set up the business thing in the Isle of Man?'

'You're as good as ever,' Paluzzi smiled. 'But I blame myself. I gave you all the information you needed to assemble the landscape, eh? Yes,' he mumbled, his expression growing vague, faraway. 'I hoped to set up here again, give myself a safe base here. I have a friend or two in the Isle of Man and it all made such beautiful sense. I was being fair to the Robertson team, but now – ' He sighed. 'I think it would be best to suspend investments for a while. My cover is broken up. This squad man Hackett – ' He closed his eyes meditatively. 'Can't recall him. I didn't know the squad bore grudges.' He chuckled to himself and got up.

'What will you – we – do?' Serena asked breathlessly. 'Will there be trouble over him?'

'I think not. No one'll know he's gone for a few days. I'll take the body to Newbury, get rid of it there. Then I'll go ahead with the ransom swap. I can do that quite easily, using a few cut-outs, a few middlemen. I can pay them off then and act as if everything is going ahead fine. Then you and me, we'll pull out, head for Paris and we'll take all the cash with us, eh? No Robertson, no one else. All for us. Then I can sit on it, wait till I find someone to launder it again for me.'

'You'd never get it out of the country.'

'Wait 'n see, girl. I've got plenty of contacts in the transport line now – and cross-Channel traffic is the easiest to smuggle on, specially the boats to France. Walkover.'

'When does the ransom go through?'

Paluzzi was leaning over Serena's dressing mirror, smearing cold cream on his damaged eyelid. 'We're as good as home and dry,' he said buoyantly. 'The demand is already through, the wheels are in motion. In twenty-four hours we'll be away.'

At lunchtime on Sunday a meeting arranged to succeed the early morning Home Office conference in Dean Ryle Street was convened in police headquarters. Hackett had expected a small turn-out but the Chief Constable – never a man for quiet ceremony – had invited every senior man concerned – officers from several departments and of varying rank. When Hackett arrived, belatedly because he had been discussing strategy with Tate, Havelock had the floor and was summarising the ransom demands. Hackett sat beside Burgess.

'A phone call to the Yard told us early this morning where to pick up certain 'information'. This turned out to be a letter, rigged up from standard newspaper cuttings, and found in a phone box, under loose flooring, in Farnborough. To cut a long story short, the demand, unsigned – ' He coughed grimly, ' – is for seven hundred and fifty thousand pounds, and it's addressed to the Greek Government, care of the Yard.' He grinned dully. 'Nice touch, that. Anyway, the Home Secretary's informal meeting settled a few things. On the Chief Constable's request, via Hackett here, the Greeks have agreed to play along with the demand. Which means we wait till the next contact – which has been promised for today – and run willingly with whatever is demanded. There has been no request to confirm – by notice in a newspaper or whatever – that we are going with the deal, so we assume our villain is assumptive of a quick job on our behalf and will act fast himself now.' Havelock's eyes set on Hackett. 'This chap feels sure he'll win,' he said slowly. 'The money is from a bank down the road, courtesy of the Treasury agent, and it's being prepared now and – in case anything should go wrong, from past experience – we are intending to micro-film all notes. If we have time.

'Now, you all know of Hackett's breaks, and he has the bit in his teeth on this one. He has an in with Stan Abney's girl and he's running her. What we have now is a possible connect with Abney sometime today – so this might bring the show to an early conclusion for us.' Havelock extended a hand to Hackett. 'If you'd give us a run-down on your plans, Hackett?' Nodding, Hackett stood.

'Right. Well, we can take it Paluzzi's our man and he's at it alone. That's his style. The hit was co-ordinated and done by the kidnap team. We can't be definitely sure who was and wasn't in. Certainly Abney, Gifford and Robertson, who, with Paluzzi will have worked out tactics. The President scare was the diversion – typical Mafia stuff – and the intention will be to use some legit process to 'clean' the ransom cash. Paluzzi's believed to have done this kind of thing before and he's good at these nice businessman covers. What his front is, we can only guess at. But we do know he may not get to the ransom swap. We know – from this Morse girl – that Abney wants to try a double-cross, to take the gear and sell it to some American head. The difficulty is, there is no direct communication between Abney and Paluzzi – I've established that definitely from the girl. We don't know if Abney knows how fast Paluzzi is working, so there's a danger of Abney's move coming too late – ' Hackett went on to give a fuller account of the background to his unearthing the Abney plot. 'Quite clearly,' he went on, 'We can go along with the girl, meet

Abney and pull him in. But he may not spill and we may lose Paluzzi and the cash. Time is the vital factor and we just don't know what we've got. Because of what we're left with the obvious action: go as far as we can with Abney without making him panic and run, *plus* play along with the ransom deal. There is every likelihood that Abney will bring us to Paluzzi or his cover house, but there's a chance he won't. Paluzzi, like all good nobs, works in very closed compartments. Trigger men like Abney have probably never even met him, so we need to be careful about the swap. Our main target is Paluzzi and we don't want to cock him up.'

'Hackett's intention,' Havelock intruded bluntly, 'is to pass one of the Squad men on to Abney as a lorry driver – a man on the regular London-Dublin run – who'd be prepared, for a fee, to take unspecified cargo to Ireland. We've fixed up the loan of a lorry there, thanks to the ACC, and hopefully we'll get a straightforward break to the goods, and maybe to Paluzzi's cover. The squad man can communicate his locations or destinations to us quite easily if the pass-off works okay.' Havelock glanced to Hackett for affirmation.

Hackett nodded. 'Detective Sergeant Bonney's a good all-round driver. He's our man. The lorry is ready 'n waiting.'

'What about the ransom hand-over?' the Chief Constable asked glumly. 'Intending to play that on the standard follow basis?' A babble of agreement rose around the room.

'About fifteen cars,' Hackett said. 'Carefully placed round the hand-over spot, wherever that might be. A good communications net. There's a 'copter – the one we always use – on stand-by to trail the collecting car if terrain is awkward. We'll presume cut-outs will be used, so we'll have to be wary of exchanges from man to man along the route.'

'Is it likely to be London or here?' Burgess asked tersely.

Hackett took him up. 'God knows. Abney's word, from the Morse girl, that he wants a driver on the London-Dublin run might suggest the gear is stocked away in, say, the general M1 or Birmingham area – so the swap might be that far away. On the other hand she believes Gifford and Abney were staying here in the city, so the deal could go here. Then the first note in Farnborough – well, that could mean London. From my point of view, I'm preparing to cover all that area. I've chalked up a list of seven 'command posts' which will be referred to as Area One, Area Two, and so on. Each of these bases are in convenient airfields or farms ranging as far apart as the Kent Downs and Cheltenham. Our ransom hand-over will be directed from the Area base nearest the requested contact spot. Right now I have cars checking each site out, making certain they're adaptable.'

'Whichever way it turns out,' the Chief Constable cut in, 'You'll have the full support of the Yard and the Divisions. And the Greeks have been most patient, very helpful.'

Sitting silently by the window, bathing his face in a stream of strong sunlight, Tate listened to everything said with little responding expression. Now he plucked the pipe from his mouth and said loudly, 'I think Hackett's priorities here are dead right. We stand a good chance, through Abney, of getting the gear and rounding up the team. But Paluzzi is the big noise, he's the one we want to be sure to get. He's been sailing away for thirty bloody years and somewhere he's got to be stopped.'

'Does he know we're on to him, do you reckon?' Burgess said.

Hackett laughed dryly. 'This is why we don't want pictures in the papers. If he's twigged us he's probably busy fortifying his cover, maybe getting set to run. I wouldn't like to be some poor bugger compromised in the middle – 'cause Paluzzi'll put down anyone who links him with this hit without compunction. Just wait 'n' see.'

No one joined in Hackett's laugh. The Chief Constable consulted his watch. He stretched in his chair. 'I've to meet the Greek attaché again at two,' he said. 'Perhaps Hackett'd give everyone an idea of contingency plans and of Bonney's proposed movements?'

Hackett leant forward. 'The meet is set for four-thirty at the tube station in Gloucester Road. . . .'

8

A clammy, oil-smelling breeze gusted down the underground tunnel every few minutes drawing Bonney and Dink closer together on the chipped wooden bench. It was 4.25.

Neither had spoken for the fifteen minutes they had been in the station and, in the few moments of distraction from the job at hand, Bonney admitted to himself sourly that Dink was a disappointment as the personification of a masseuse. He had expected a siren, a robust little hoyden who'd wear bright red lipstick, deep V-neck clothes no matter what the weather, and would display huge expanses of suspendered thigh at every opportunity. Instead, Dink looked more like the buttoned-up crusaders who sing songs about lost souls and finding God. Her clothes were plain, even prim, and the beige wool coat she sported covered her knees and gave no secrets away. And to top that, except for a few whispered words with Hackett during the run from Putney, she had had nothing at all to say to him. On the way to the tube he had tried to warm her up conversationally, but her monosyllabic replies had finally defeated him. He supposed – quite rightly – she was nervous of what she had to do.

'You sure he'll show?' Bonney said, seeing the time creeping up to the half-hour.

Dink shrugged. She didn't want to think about it. Hackett had carefully justified it to her, explaining pros and cons, and his persuasiveness had made her feel good. But when the initial impact of his argument wore off the whole affair seemed too much like treachery to be borne.

She had actively considered quitting on him, running away before he called at the arranged time, but that wasn't her style. She prided herself on her courage and tenacity, and had always boasted – truthfully – that she never shirked responsibilities. Aside from the personalities involved, aside from the moral issue (though she didn't dwell on that), what she was doing was shrewd and wise since, according to Hackett, it was Stan's only chance of some diminution of charges. Briefly, seated in the biting chill with Bonney, Dink wondered had Hackett lied to her. Was it possible that he didn't really know where Stan was? Maybe the Bond Street information had come to him from some small fish in the underworld who knew him? Maybe it was all a ruse, all the tough talk and then the smooth 'afters'?

'Here he is. Know that mug anywhere.' Bonney was shifting uncomfortably beside her. The District line train from Richmond had come in and a sparse group of passengers had alighted.

Abney strode up, looking drawn and tired. His sandy hair had been cut tight since the D/F photo, Bonney saw, and the jowls looked flabby now, but otherwise the lop-sided handsome face was unchanged. He stooped down and kissed Dink on the top of her head, his eyes angling to Bonney. Dink asked was everything all right. A superfluous question in the circumstances, Bonney thought good-humouredly. Abney didn't think so.

'It's old Giff – you know?' he said in a hushed tone barely audible to Bonney. 'Vanished. Left me a note saying he'd gone to see the top man. Said he'd ring before twelve.'

'So – ? He didn't ring?' Dink's voice was edgy, rough – manifestly unnatural to Bonney's ears. Mentally he resolved to get rid of her, as Hackett had advised, as soon as he could.

'No, he didn't call. Unlike him. He was going to look for cash. Hope he didn't cause a stir – for his own sake and for ours. The poor bugger was very het up – said he'd get the law in if the top man didn't fix it for him. He was cut up about the follows, the pressure.'

'Big deal. Doesn't affect you.'

'Will if he blows the gaff. And the way he is, I wouldn't be surpised if he did. This Julie's friend?'

'Lewis,' Bonney said, putting a hand out.

'What company?' Abney didn't take the hand. His expression was dark, but more troubled than hostile.

'T & C Scott Europe Services.'

'What do you do?'

'Drive a truck.'

'Funny.' Abney smiled stiffly, new interest coming into his face. Bonney cringed inwardly. He hadn't intended to rile Abney in any way. 'Look, son, I presume my little lady here told you want I want – eh? Good – then let's talk in specifics. Are you on a regular run?'

'Yeah. Trunking. We supply tractors and trailers for other people's gear. But runs vary.'

Abney turned to Dink suddenly. Abstracted, Dink gave a start. 'You never told me you'd pals in the moving trade,' he said.

'I remembered him. Julie said he did some work for the Germans, the people who own the parlour.'

Abney nodded. He eyed Bonney slowly up and down, considering. 'Want to go somewhere for a cuppa?'

Bonney shook his head. 'Haven't got much time. What exactly do you want me to carry?' That sounded sweetly naïve. Abney's grin reflected that. He didn't answer but turned back to Dink. 'I want to chat to this fella,' he said. 'Better if you went for a walk.'

'You're going back to the club, aren't you, Dink?' Bonney put in interestedly. Dink looked momentarily flustered. Then she nodded rapidly. 'Oh yeah. I said I'd relieve Julie, didn't I?'

The tangle of lies seemed to sail over Abney's head. Politely escorting Dink up the steps to the exit he thanked her for the lucky introduction and asked her about Hackett. Dink gave blunt, careful answers and spoke no more than she had to, but Abney failed to recognise the spurious formality of her talk. He seemed excited at the prospects of making a quick deal with this 'Lewis'. At the exit he stalled with her as Bonney kicked his heels on the steps.

'This is c.o.d. – so I won't have the loot till I get going. I'll send you something to come over to Ireland – okay?' His tone was half-interested. She knew that the spirit of the conspiracy had him, body and soul, now. His bet was down and the wheel was spinning. He was in for the win – only the win.

With a quick word of good-bye she left, a curious trill of pleasure ringing like a victory bell in her ears, drowning the thumping beat of her heart. For better or worse, the trick had succeeded. Abney was in Hackett's hands now.

Rejoining Bonney, Abney led him up to the street and they started sauntering idly, sticking to the main routes and avoiding crowds.

'What's your tractor?' Abney asked.

'I'm driving a unit now,' Bonney said casually. 'Scania tractor. Three of us alternate runs to Ireland, picking up various stocks from various firms. I usually go Monday and Wednesday.'

'Same stocks each time?'

'No. Sometimes fridges, sometimes groupage. You never know.'

'When's your next run?'

'Tonight, then Wednesday. I'm taking a small load – household implements – to Holyhead.'

'And where's your lorry now?'

'Loading. It'll be loaded for me and I'll pick it up

tonight. In Slough.' Bonney looked sharply at Abney. 'Why?' he asked. 'How soon do you want this load to move? I'll have to put a bit of thought into it.'

'Thought my arse. I'll give you a grand in Dublin.'

'For what?'

Abney sucked in air noisily. He wasn't about to commit himself so easily. 'Important papers,' he said. 'Two crates. Not heavy. I'll load them myself, tell you where to come. It won't be too far off your Holyhead run.'

'For a grand?' Bonney chuckled. 'I'll do the Library Association for a grand. Wednesday suit you?'

'Tonight'd suit me better. I don't have time to waste.'

'Tonight's a bit of a hassle.'

'I could help you. The loading and unloading'll be simple. If you got a start from Slough an hour earlier you'd be flying, no problems.'

Bonney fell to silence for a minute and Abney was suddenly garrulous and cheery. He had plenty of friends in the business but it was hard to know the real trustworthy ones, he said. Two many times before he had been cheated and he had become suspicious of honour and confidence. He wanted to give a break to a new man.

'All right,' Bonney conceded. 'I'll take your stuff. Where do I load up?'

Abney slapped him curtly on the shoulder. 'Good lad. Meet me this evening – what time are you off from Holyhead?'

'Two o'clock tomorrow afternoon. But it's a ten-hour drive.'

'Right, well – you got a piece of paper?'

Bonney nodded and took out a bar of chocolate. He peeled off the wrapper and jotted down the address of a pub in Reading dictated by Abney. 'I'll be there just before closing time,' Abney told him. 'Come through to the public bar and I'll join you. Presumably you'll have the lorry ready plus Cargo Manifest and all?'

Expecting this kind of 'plumbing' talk, Bonney had taken the trouble of being briefed by a transport manager and he knew what travel papers were needed. For a few minutes he chatted authoritatively about Consignment Notes and possible Customs dangers. Impressed, Abney vented his satisfaction by inviting him for a drink and a meal; but Bonney declined deftly, saying he had family to visit in town.

As Abney led Bonney back to the tube Bonney said, 'There won't be any trouble from anyone here, will there? I mean, this gear isn't stolen?' The questions, he knew, were laden, deadly – but Abney seemed relaxed enough to chance them on him. They might, Bonney guessed, give some indication of the balance of his relationship with Paluzzi.

Abney laughed. 'Stolen? Who'd deal in dirty goods. No,' he said smoothly. 'They'll be okay. I might have to . . . . well, sneak 'em out of a certain friend's place. But, I assure you – they're all mine. But anyway – ' He stopped in front of Bonney as they came to Gloucester Road tube entrance. 'The grand'll ease your conscience, won't it?'

Bonney feigned a careless look. 'Okay then. See you tonight.'

'Right.' Abney went to move away, checked his step and called after Bonney. 'Just thinking,' he said slowly. 'Since the gear'll go all right in your lorry, why can't I go?'

'I'm not allowed to take passengers.'

'Not in the cab, sonny. In with the gear. That's fair indemnity, ain't it? I'm sure the gear gets there. You're sure of your cash.'

'I don't mind taking the chance on the boat,' Bonney said, 'once there's no trouble loading the stuff. I don't feel like getting knocked over the head.'

'There'll be no trouble. Anyone else who's involved, I

can handle.'

'So there'll be others?'

Abney stared lifelessly at Bonney, reluctantly estimating obstacles, Bonney guessed. 'Leave the worrying to me,' he said.

The telephone jangling, reverberating against the exotic table lamp of sham Lalique glass woke Paluzzi from a dreamless sleep, lying between Serena's legs. He didn't change his posture, just grated his pelvic bone into her stomach to wake her and leant over to take the receiver. Robertson's voice tripped down the line.

'Everything's set. Two cut-outs fixed.'

Paluzzi was angry with Robertson but the telephone, experience told, was not a safe method of arguing a toss. 'All right,' he said. 'I'll be down this evening. Await my contact. The first demand's gone through.'

'The radio didn't carry it.'

'Didn't expect it to. They'll bide their time.'

He rang off. Serena lay inert, her eyes closed but the pupils beneath not stirring. Paluzzi smiled. Quite apart from sexual activity, bed was his favourite testing ground for women. In a long voracious sex life he had known many women of all ages and had come to nurse a belief that inhibitions and affectations drop away like autumn leaves once clothes are shed and bed play begins. No woman *acted* well in bed. A faithful woman *feels* faithful in the grip of her thighs and the openness of her passion; a con trickster *feels* phoney. And now, bedding Serena for the first time in all those years, the mantle of hauteur had fallen away and he had got an insight to her soul. She was like a child, he saw – timid and hungry for loving. Her response to him had been exertive, urgent. She had wanted desperately to satisfy him.

A tiny frown puckered his brow. It hadn't hit him till now – but, could it be that her enthusiasm was fired by fear? She had been trembling when he undressed her and pulled her to bed – was that the excitement of love, or reaction to the killing? Fear, Paluzzi felt, was never an acceptable basis for intimate relationships. It was a danger. Fear destoryed trust: the Mafia knew that, it was part of their code.

Paluzzi blew gently on Serena's eyelids, but they didn't move. Then, lowering himself on her, his teeth gripped the nylon top of her bra and edged it down. Her right breast, large and firm, stood exposed. For a minute he kissed the pale skin of the upper chest, then his mouth found the slope of the bust and he slid down. Very slowly his teeth enclosed the nipple and bit hard. Serena jerked away from him, her eyes blazing, but his grip around her waist was too tight and he held her down.

'Did you enjoy that?' he said, smiling.

'I like sex,' she said, her hands placing themselves on his shoulders. Restraining or embracing?

'It's good for you – and me,' he grinned. 'It's my exercise before the million dollar deal, eh? Like athletes train for a race – with love-making before the big event.' When she said nothing he moved on: 'You give in very easy to me,' he said.

'We're old friends. I gave in to you a long time ago.'

Paluzzi watched her closely for several minutes. In the back of his mind her words, her whole attitude, was bothering him. There was an indefinable strength in the girl which was irksome. Six years ago he had detected it, but it had been more subtle then, more manageable.

'Anyway,' he said. 'Sex is a great lenitive – soothes away all worries.'

'I'm not worried anymore,' she said tersely. She touched his forehead, ran a thumb across his right eyebrow. 'But you must get that burn seen to. It may go septic. I'll put more cream on it.' In a single writhing movement she pushed Paluzzi off and climbed out of bed. Dispassionately he watched her walk naked to the dresser by the window. The splendid body, coloured like creamy coffee with bright pallor highlighting the fun places, triggered a fresh spring of interest in him. Serena had so much more to give, he reflected. If only that stubborn spirit was laid to rest. If only she *gave* more, went along with him . . . .

'When will you take the body away?' she said, her face away from him, the words atonal.

'An hour. It'll be dark by seven. Won't be so suspicious. I can drive round the back and take him out that way. I'll be driving up to Newbury then, staying at the house I rented.'

'Not the warehouse?'

'My good friend Robertson's there, looking after the goods. We start the swap – cash for the bronze – first thing in the morning.'

'How'll you do it – the swap, I mean?'

'Give the police, who no doubt'll be directing affairs, a paperchase of leads – get them to hand the cash over to a cut-out – put him on a roundabout route – then put the Greek stuff in a van, stolen by King specially for the occasion – and ring 'em to say where it is. Very easy.'

'How long will all that take?'

'Four, five hours. I'll start at midnight or so because I want no traffic and darkness for the swap, if possible.'

'I presume it's up to this Robertson to hand over the stuff, in the van?'

'I'll be leaving most of the messy work to him.' Paluzzi became sullen. 'Pity 'bout him. He could've been a really good man. A little discipline – ' Paluzzi shrugged. 'They don't make 'em like they used to.' He thought of Hackett. 'Or maybe they do,' he mumbled.

Serena applied cream to his face, then walked off to the bathroom to shower. Paluzzi ambled in after her and sat outside the frosted glass partition. 'I feel this is going to be a perfect success despite the problems,' he said. 'All we need is a good wrap-up. You can tell your stewards you are going for a holiday, that you've a sick relative in the country – some story. I'll get tickets to France. We can fly out tomorrow night. Your passport is okay? No endorsements?'

'Yes. My passport is fine.'

'Good. Then I need only look after my own. Excellent.'

'Could we not put off the going for a day or two? Maybe I could join you later?'

The glass door rattled open. Paluzzi reached into the shower and took her arm. He pulled her streaming wet body from the spray and held her close. His eyes were bright, the burnt one drawn open, hideous and purple-shot. 'You're not happy with my plans?' he said – the gravity of his voice impossible to weigh.

'N-no. It's just that I don't know if I want to . . . . I like it here . . . . but, if I go . . . . everyone would be suspicious if I rushed off.'

'But you wanted in. You said so. You followed me to Newbury to say so.'

'I wanted to know what you were involved in – that's all. It's nothing to do with me.'

Paluzzi's expression became sympathetic and kind. 'I think you're distraught because of old Gifford, eh? You should take a sleeping pill and skip tonight's shift. Do you good. In the morning I'll call for you.' He kissed her roughly on the lips and helped her stand back under the shower.

Ten minutes later, warmly clad against the cold, Paluzzi pushed into the bathroom again. Serena was propped on the vanity chair beside the tri-mirror, a dressing-gown draped about her, spreading almond oil on her feet and legs. 'I've to bring the car round,' he said. 'And I've a phone call to make. Won't be fifteen minutes.' He closed the door softly and descended the stairs to the little hallway. Before going into the street he paused in the crouching darkness and thought.

Things hadn't gone well. The Crime Squad bastard was on to him – even before the hit seemingly – and the team were proving to be a ramshackle group. There were too many security risks in Robertson's careless methods. The Isle of Man company that he had intended to confide only to Robertson was apparently known by everyone now. Whatever for the team, the girl Serena was not to be trusted. He couldn't just leave her. He would have to take her or . . . .

The siren scream of a passing ambulance startled him from his musings and he grabbed the collar of his coat tightly round his chin and dismissed the thoughts. He went out into the cold.

Hackett, Bonney and Louise sat in the gathering gloom of a secluded corner of the Wechester Arms, dining on stewed coffee and fish-paste sandwiches.

'When I make contact in Reading you'll stick up close for a follow?' Bonney was saying.

Hackett nodded. 'We'll do what we can, but there's real risks – you know that. Abney's bound to be itchy once he's headed for the gear.'

'I could take a walkie-talkie in case.'

'No. Right out. What happens if he gets suspicious and checks you? Stay clean. If we don't show at the warehouse use some stall to phone. Tell him you've forgotten the What's-its-name Manifest. I'll clear a line for you with the Yard, and they can buzz me then – right? All you need do is give an indication of your whereabouts.'

'How in Christ do I do that with him maybe at my elbow?'

'Use your wooden box, kiddo. Say you want Manifest Number M18 – motorway junction 8 – or A3415 – fifteen miles from Reading on the A34. Some simple code – try and be as accurate as possible.'

'But you may not find it on a code. And I may not be able to phone from the warehouse.'

'So? You phone from ten miles up the road. What difference will it make? We'll pull you in, take Abney. After that we can back-track to this warehouse and see what we can get to Paluzzi. Once he takes you to the warehouse – that's the big thing. For starters, it gives us a million's worth of goodies back.'

'And if I don't get to a phone? – there's always an outside chance. If I'm not armed, it might be difficult to take Abney myself.'

'Don't worry, Blue Eyes. We'll tip Holyhead in case worse comes to worst. You won't be cast adrift on the high seas. Main thing for you is, concentrate on making Abney happy. Turn on the Jimmy Cagney.'

Bonney eyed Hackett depreciatively. This high good humour would keep Hackett now till the job concluded, he knew. Hackett was basically a man of war and when, for a long period there was no action, his whole being went into decline. But now the ranks were forming and battle was about to begin. Nothing could suppress the ebullience that would give rise to in Hackett. Bonney envied his boss's composed optimism. He trusted the intelligence of Hackett's planning, but he was also wary of the inevitable snags in a run like this. Hackett would be equally aware of the danger areas, would have given them lengthy thought, assembled counter-moves; but now, with the game in play, he would avoid mulling over them.

'How about the swap?' Bonney said. 'Any news?'

Hackett shrugged. He turned to Louise. 'Now that Bonney's revived it, luv – go and call the office. Ask if anything's in.' Louise deserted her coffee and marched off.

'We've gone through several little men,' Hackett said. 'The likely cut-out material. I had Lennie do all our old friends, but we came up with nothing. What's against us is location. We're off our stroke 'cause we don't know if the swap'll be here or in Birmingham or Southampton. No way of knowing.'

'You reckon Paluzzi's at this warehouse, where the stuff's hoarded?'

'Doubt it, if we know Paluzzi. I doubt if Abney'd have an idea where he is even.'

'So what happens when Abney nicks the gear and we nick him? If the warehouse doesn't give us Paluzzi?'

'Well, I'm not goin' in with six bloody guns blazing, am I? We'll keep it low, suss out what kind of a business is running there and who's boss. Could be Paluzzi's own venture. Then again, could be a mate of one of the team.' Hackett knocked back the last of his coffee and sat back. His voice became introverted, low. 'This is the closest we've ever got to that bastard. I'm not letting this one go. Paluzzi won't be the first cowboy whose misjudgement of cronies landed him in it.'

'Abney's a help.'

'Dink was a help,' Hackett said flatly, focussing back on Bonney.

'The tart with the heart.' Bonney smiled.

'Maybe,' Hackett grimaced, non-committal. 'Poor old Stan chose the wrong lay for a life in crime, that's for sure. Dink sees reason too easily.' He pulled a swaggering face. 'And succumbs too easily to good-looking men.'

'Yeah,' Bonney said, straight-faced. 'Like Abney. Very Errol Flynn.'

They both glanced up quickly as Louise appeared suddenly beside them. The news was conveyed by her eyes before she spoke.

'Another contact?' Hackett said.

'Phone call. To the Greek Embassy this time. About the packing of the money.'

'How does he want it?'

'Six leather bags. Hundreds and fifties only.'

'When?'

'No word yet.'

'Big currency notes,' Hackett mumbled. 'I wonder is he getting set to travel.'

Leaving his Mercedes parked in the masking cover of a leafy copse near the perimeter fence, Paluzzi stumbled through the pitch darkness of a moonless night with the massive weight of Gifford's spent body over his shoulder and staggered into the rear entrance to the 'Whiteline' warehouse that abutted onto the office building. No light showed from the office window but Paluzzi knew this was because thick blackout paper had been pasted up by Robertson. Now, at a quarter-to-eleven, he knew Robertson would be in there, killing time, waiting . . .

Inside, the spacious warehouse which had once been a well-fitted garage was empty and neat, except for the skeleton of a long-expired Ford tractor, erected and abandoned on a repair ramp, and some twenty stacked wooden boxes lined up by the far wall. A dried-up tarpaulin, perforated and friable with age, lay near these. Without hesitation, Paluzzi took the tight-wrapped corpse over to the tarpaulin, dropped it upon the decaying material and covered it loosely. Before leaving the area, Paluzzi shinned up onto the boxes and rummaged among the topmost five. Lifting one out of the way he saw what he wanted – the

Greek-marked crates, placed neatly side-by-side and within easy access for removal. He slapped them cheerily and jumped off the stack. Then, using his keys, he locked up the warehouse and let himself into the office building. Robertson, ever vigilant, ambushed him quietly in the hallway. 'Only you,' he hissed. 'I saw the light in the jar of the warehouse door.'

'I came through the back way,' Paluzzi said dully. 'Don't want to hang round.'

Brusquely he went upstairs, moved into the office and immediately poured himself a brandy from what was patently Robertson's supper-time ration array. Robertson followed him in, sat behind the desk and resumed eating his cold pie. Surreptitiously, from the tail of his eye, Robertson watched Paluzzi agitatedly move around the room. He wondered what was troubling him but guessed it was probably just the excitement of the closing stages of a meaty deal.

Paluzzi was excited, but not nearly as much as Robertson estimated. The tension that gripped him grew from his frustration in dealing with half-competent, half-trustworthy people like Robertson. During the drive north he had contemplated the idea of confronting Robertson, underlining his deficiencies, his deadly mistakes. But, when everything was balanced up, it seemed a wasteful idea. There was nothing to be achieved by arguing with Robertson and the mistakes were impossible to redress anyway. Far better to conserve energies and maintain a surface calm.

'These cut-outs,' Paluzzi said evenly, 'are they good men?'

'Sound. No quitters. They don't know what they're taking, so they'll be cool. But cautious – don't worry.'

'I want the first man out in two hours. I'm going to put the call through at twelve-thirty. The pick-up will be in Savernake Forest. The darkness will help and the man – as we arranged – is to be on a motorbike. Is that sorted out?'

'Yes. He's got a Suzuki. Medium bike, picked it up in Kingsclere and – '

'Right. I'll phone you with the exact pick-up point at, say, two. You have him at his post waiting. You ring him and tell him where to go. Then alert the second man. One passes to the other – neither men knowing each other, of course – ' Robertson nodded. 'The second man leaves the cash at the barn we found. Goes to that kiosk and rings you. You drive to it, get it. Give it twenty minutes, then take the bronze stuff in the stolen van, dump it in Newbury. You still have it under wraps, I presume?'

'It's down behind the old Volvo in the yard, looks fine. New plates.'

'Good. Then we are ready.' Paluzzi clapped his hands like a circus ringmaster. He grinned humourlessly to Robertson who found the crooked stare disquieting. The marked eye registered with him but, since Paluzzi hadn't offered explanation, he didn't ask for it. 'You're in a bit of a rush to see this through, aren't you?' he said, mustering as much geniality into the question as possible.

Paluzzi stood, quite motionless, and stared over at him. After a long time he said, 'I'm getting old, you know. The kind of miscalculations I've made this time would never have been tolerable before. In the old days, in New York, you'd get a splash of eserine in your coffee for that.'

'What kind of miscalculation?' Robertson said, genuinely surprised. 'From our end everything went all right.'

Paluzzi sighed in a heartfelt, weary manner. 'I think maybe standards differ, no?' He brushed the sombre mood off. 'The girl Serena is not reliable.'

'I told you that,' Robertson said, relieved. For a moment he had thought some criticism had been aimed at him. But for what? Abney's phone call of yesterday had tripped through his head: Abney said the Crime Squad were on to each of them, hounding their families. Maybe the Jag had been spotted by that woman on the slip-road, maybe she had recognised his face.

'I'm not happy about leaving her around. She is unstable.'

'Well – ' Robertson suddenly knew what Paluzzi was saying. Instinct told him to manoeuvre out of it. He was in enough entangled trouble at the moment. 'Bring her with you,' he suggested.

'No. I don't want to go back there. You do her for me.'

'But I thought you wanted me to stay here?'

'Now that it's ending, you can move. Drive down tomorrow. You know where the club is.' Paluzzi saw Robertson's unease. He pushed on convincingly. 'There'll be a small extra whack for it, I promise you.'

'And a run out of the country?'

'Of course.'

Robertson stood up, swept the crumbs of his meal to one side and scrubbed his face tiredly, thinking. 'All right,' he said. 'I'll do it in the morning. I suppose sooner the better.'

'Good, then. And I'll leave it to your good judgement to dispose of the body.'

'Fine. How about the money then?'

'Money?'

'Yeah.' Robertson laughed. 'When do we get cuts? You had suggested we meet in the club tomorrow afternoon.'

'Well, let's get it first. Then tomorrow – ' He fixed a happy smile on his lips. 'You come to my house, the rented house, and we'll arrange whacks. Say one o'clock – all right? Give me time to get some sleep.'

Agreements reached, Paluzzi shook Robertson's hand, wishing him luck, then told him to call the first cut-out and put him on stand-by now. Then, going back the way he had arrived, he retraced his steps to the warehouse and bundled

Gifford's body into the dilapidated Ford on the ramp and carefully covered it with various pieces of junk. The likelihood of Robertson finding it there would be very slender, and tomorrow it wouldn't matter anyway.

Paluzzi ran back to the Mercedes with a laden mind. There was so much to do. Passage for the money would have to be set up. There was an Italian who worked out of Dover would help out there. And himself – he would have to look after a solo run out of Britain. He could chance a faked passport, but it might prove awkward if this Hackett character had been doing his footwork exercises properly. Maybe it would be better to let the Italian shipping man do the lot. For fifty grand a good job would be guaranteed. The dangers of marked money reared up in his mind and he cursed out loud. It could have been so simple with the company in the Isle of Man – just a case of slipping investments in and waiting for maturing, clean-money returns. Now, the three-quarters of a million would fetch only maybe a quarter in negotiable cash.

But a quarter was something. The hit would be thirty-three per cent successful. This time at least, the stigma of failure in Britain would be quenched.

9

Twenty minutes after Bonney had entered the Reading pub there was still no sign of him emerging.

Hackett, seated with Louise in the Capri, conspicuously parked at a bottleneck – the only passable viewing point – two hundred yards away, had become impatient. Louise sat quite motionless in the darkness while Hackett discoursed with acerbity. What could Bonney be doing? Drinking? The bastard was delaying things. Time was important. What if Paluzzi started the swap? He could move the gear and Abney might never get it – *they* might not get it. Was Abney even in the pub yet? Look, for God's sake – Bonney'd even parked the thirteen-ton truck blocking a car park exit!

Louise gave way to a giggle. Hackett's outbursts at times like these were always airy, irrational and downright entertaining. Not one iota was meant to be taken seriously and most of the Crime Squad knew the legends of the Hackett temperament and took steps accordingly to either shut their minds off while working a follow with him or avoid teaming at all. But Louise in particular was impervious to the chronic chatter and, if anything, its staccato drone relaxed her, shattering the tensions that gathered in quietude.

From time to time people leaving the pub and a hotel next door to it strolled up the street, passing in single file on the narrowed tow-path beside the car. Conscious of looking suspicious, Hackett leant over and hooked his arms round Louise in a convincingly passionate clinch. His angry commentary ceased abruptly. Louise, her head cradled on his shoulder, said, 'I'll bet you parked here on purpose.'

'Not at all. I grin and bear it,' Hackett quipped. 'Remember – we're doing this for Queen and country.' His grip tightened, his breath blowing through her hair. Another time, Louise thought vaguely, present circumstances would make a worthwhile game. She arched her back and sank more comfortably into Hackett.

Just then Bonney came out of the pub. The tall figure of Abney, dressed, like Bonney, in casual clothes, was instantly recognised by Louise and Hackett. 'At last – the opposition,' Hackett said very gently. Louise felt his body go rigid and his pace of breathing speeded.

Walking fast, Bonney and Abney crossed to the lorry, clambered in and started off. Abney, Hackett clearly observed, was nervy and, before getting into the cab he looked carefully in through the canvas cover on one side of the trailer. Hackett gave them a three minute start. Before following he radioed the first of two other cars and informed them the Scania was headed west.

At a little after eleven o'clock he was motoring slowly along back-roads from Reading, stalling intermittently but keeping the truck in sight. Traffic on the roads was predictably heavy enough, with late night revellers heading homewards, and that suited Hackett well enough. The UHF crackled. 'Hackett, One – headed west A329 – confirm?'

'He's off route,' Louise said. 'Will I call him in?'

Hackett said no. 'He's running almost parallel with us, so if the lorry finds the main road again he'll pick it up easy enough. Where's Two?'

Louise clicked the radio on and called Two. It promptly gave a satisfactory position, trailing at a half mile, following Hackett. 'Looks like he's going north,' Louise commented. 'Towards where – Nettlebed? Oxford?'

'Could be. Bonney's keeping a happy pace.'

The truck was travelling quite fast for the cramped country lanes it was now among. The further into the country they went, the fewer cars there were and Hackett was forced to pull back considerably, making quick advances only when, sometimes for longish periods, the thick hedges that fringed the road ate up the truck. Twice they seemed to lose it completely and Hackett accelerated wildly to catch up.

'That's probably Abney's orders,' Hackett observed. 'Taking no chances. He could be taking Bonney on a roundabout run.' He took up the radio again and asked Two to join him now. 'How's location?' he said to Louise. Louise checked the map on her lap with a pencil-beam torch. 'All right,' she said. Coming near the 4074 junction.'

'Make sure we don't lose One.'

Louise took the radio and called One. 'Stick to 329 north now,' Louise ordered. One confirmed. Headlights behind them flashed blindingly. The UHF roared loud. 'Two behind you now. Overtake?'

The lorry was out of sight again. No harm for Hackett to drop back for a while. 'Okay. On you go,' Hackett said. He jabbed the brakes, saw the grey Chrysler shoot on ahead of him, the two bland faces turning towards him in brief acknowledgement. He waved to them, handed the radio to Louise and slowed back to thirty.

'Do you think Abney's on to Bonney?' Louise said.

'Abney's a grabber. He's crazy to get that cash. He'll have reservations about old Bonney, but he'll trust him.' He frowned in the dark. 'I hope.'

The UHF drowned Louise's retort. 'Two – Hackett? He's not up here.'

Hackett's heart winged. He was up ahead five minutes ago, trundling regularly at fifty. 'Repeat!' Hackett barked.

'Not here. I'm way up.'

Hackett crashed back a gear and darted forward. Christ, it was impossible! Where could it have turned off? Had they passed any forks? No, certainly nothing major. 'Map?' he half-shouted to Louise. Louise scanned the network of roads ahead. 'Nothing. We're turned north-east now, towards Watlington. No junctions up ahead. Unless he belted it and made the next crossroads.'

'How far?'

'Four miles.'

'No, unlikely.'. He lifted the radio. 'Two, get right up, far as it goes – report anything.'

'Could've pulled round – in a farm gate – and doubled back. Lights out, we'd never have noticed.'

'All supposing Abney's bloody suspicious-minded,' Hackett snapped. He called One on the UHF and asked them to take the B4009 and drive back the route they had just come.

Having covered almost three miles now without catching sight of either Two or the truck, Hackett braked again and rolled on slowly, examining the country around the road. Much of it was farmland, whole tracts heavily wooded. There was ample shelter, even for a forty-foot truck like Bonney's – farm tracks, bushy walks, barns. Hackett called Two again and checked their position. They had certainly moved far enough ahead now, and nothing had been seen. One, four miles back now, had nothing to report. Drawing the Capri to a halt in a silent, pitch-black road Hackett thumped the steering-wheel with both fists and shot a dozen vigorous oaths.

'They obviously turned,' Louise said. 'He must suspect Bonney.'

Hackett said nothing, slammed the car into gear and effected a careless five-point turn, constantly swearing heatedly. Racing up to a nerve-shaking ninety, Hackett relaxed into his seat. 'If Bonney's blown we're in real trouble,' he said. 'We'd better find that bloody truck.'

Not half-a-mile away Bonney's ears pricked quickly as the sound of Hackett's car shot past, fading rapidly to stillness. He knew what it meant. The squad had lost him and would probably guess Abney had tried to side-step them. But that wasn't the case. The whole thing had been coincidental misfortune. Unfamiliar with the handling of the heavy truck, Bonney had been slow with reactions to Abney's instructions. Twice he had missed narrow turnings suggested by Abney and, finally going far off route, Abney had told him to pull round at the next opening and back-track. Abney was as unsure of territory as he was and, mellowed by five whiskies in twenty-odd minutes at the pub, his eye hadn't been keen enough to notice Bonney's hesitant behaviour. The strokes of bad luck redoubled when Bonney turned onto what looked in the heavy darkness like a good-surfaced farm track. There were lights a half-mile ahead and the track had appeared to connect with a major road. Seeing no sign of the follow, Bonney decided to try the track and reconnect with the main road. He got no further than three hundred yards up the pitted road when, stalling between gears, the rear wheels found a deep furrow in the clay surface and stuck fast. Bonney's immediate reaction had been to rev the engine hard, not so much to free the twisting tyres, but to alert the follow cars. Abney, in his invective half-stupor vociferously ordered him out of the cab and together, bumping and stumbling through the Stygian night, they searched for stones and wood pieces to lay under the wheels for traction.

Now, hearing what must be last of the squad cars screaming away into the distance, a morbid gloom swamped Bonney. How would Hackett translate his disappearance? Would he think the job was blown and Abney had overpowered him? Would he think of the possibilities of errors on Bonney's behalf? The big risk was over-reaction. Anxious to establish the exact position, the squad might locate the truck again and run it too closely. But then Hackett had been aware of the likelihood of Abney being extra-cautious, so he in turn might accept the loss and play it coolly. Whichever way, for now the ball was soundly in Bonney's court. Lying on his back in the mud and grit under the wheels Bonney decided on tactics. He still had Abney in his pocket and the Greek haul, their destination, was, according to Abney, not fifteen miles away. He was homing in. Keeping Abney's confidence must be his prime consideration – getting to the stuff, that's all that mattered. With a conscious effort he turned his thoughts away from everything but Abney and the jammed truck.

'Hurry up, for Chrissake,' Abney shouted. 'We'll be late for that bloody boat if we don't get moving.'

Bonney wedged a handful of splinter wood under the nearside tyre and shut out the nudging thought that the odds for getting as far as Holyhead were shortening, getting better all the time.

'We're on!'

Hackett slipped back into the car and slammed the door. His face in the diffused glow of the dash light was orange and strange. Louise's immediate assumption from the restrained exuberance in his words was that Bonney had been located. He had pulled in at a phone kiosk to check the line to the Yard.

'Everything's moving,' he repeated. 'The swap demand's started.'

'Since when?'

As if answering theatrical cue, the UHF started blaring, calling Hackett, and the news was succinctly reiterated.

Another call to the Greek Embassy. The ransom money was to be taken to a children's playground in Andover in one hour. Only one car with one occupant was to be involved and a stern warning said the sculpture would be damaged if a tail was observed. Hackett acknowledged and replied, speaking excitedly:

'All men to Area Six. Immediately. Get the 'copter up. And take the money.'

The voice burst strongly over the radio. 'Wilco. Over to Six. Out.'

'Area Six,' Louise repeated. 'The airfield north of the town?'

Hackett nodded, firing the engine. 'Should suit us ideally,' he said. 'If time is on our side now – ' He pulled dangerously across the road, cutting the edge of a junction and joining the main road heading west.

'You think the hand-over'll be in that park?'

'No way. That's first in a chain. Gives us time to get half set-up anyway. Could be dawn, later, before the contact's made.'

'Any news on Bonney?'

The UHF flooded out again, silencing them. The message was calling individual cars to Area Six. Hackett lowered the volume. 'Bonney's in the laps of the gods,' he said. 'I'll leave Chick up behind, cruising that district, but it's probably a waste of time.' Taking the radio again he called Chick in Two and passed on the instruction.

'Do you think he's blown?'

Hackett grunted negatively. 'Abney showed his clock too easily in Reading. If he was cagey like that he'd never have got into the truck. No. I think he was cautious all right, but Bonney's too bright a boy to walk himself into one-way traps.'

'So we wait for a phone call?'

'Big problem is, maybe Paluzzi'll move the goods before

they get to them. No doubt about it – He'll hand 'em over once the cash is given. He'll dump 'em somewhere. Abney knows they've been stocked away in some warehouse. But where'll they be tonight?'

'We'll keep fingers crossed till we get that phone call.'

They motored through the sleeping town of Newbury and took the road for Andover. A majestic moon like the misted sun was rising through the woods to the east.

Through the haze of a Seconal sleep the pink piazza of a dreamland Siena suddenly materialised into the shell-shaped tail-board of Serena's bed. Shaken from sleep by an unheralded spasm of galloping heartbeats, Serena sat up on the bed and gulped air into her lungs. The alarming palpitations immediately began to recede. She sat stiffly at the edge of the bed and slipped her head between her knees.

It was usually this way when she was under strain or tired. Invariably her first recourse was to the bottle, and she always drank too much too quickly. Inexpensive Chianti made her drunk fastest – and there was always nausea afterwards – but with a kind of misplaced patriotic idealism she forsook the more prudent tranquillising drinks and stuck to it. Combined with sleeping pills, it was deadly. Nine times out of ten after a bender she slept badly and was physically sick but there were rare superbly oblivious exceptions – nights when the booze and drugs induced nirvana itself – and, like the dipper with the hookah, it was for these she went on drinking, searching.

It had been a bad idea copping out of the club tonight and turning to the bottle. Tonight, of all nights, the oblivion of booze could achieve nothing for her. Now, as she was sitting here, the seconds of her existence here were ticking away.

Paluzzi, whether she liked it or not, intended to take her

away from the club. His reasons for wanting her were ambiguous. Certainly he liked her, found her desirable; but that desire had never made him want to make commitments up to now. But now he did. Pulling off a million-dollar coup, he wanted to take her with him and leave the country. *Why?* Could Serena afford to ignore the 'security' aspect of his new enthusiasm? He had killed Gifford because he had threatened (Paluzzi alleged) to compromise him. Could it be that her knowledge of him presented a similar tacit threat in the new circumstances? If so, was his real intention merely to remove her from the scene – take her elsewhere, anywhere, where the chances of a connection to him became remote? But if that was the motive and if he didn't *want* her, what guarantee had she that in retiring formally from the club and running off with him she was not giving him the perfect facilities for a second clean sheet murder?

She had brought so much of it on herself but there was no consolation in admitting to that. She had changed in the last few years and she had wondered how much he too had altered. That was all that drove her to snooping around him, she told herself. Just curiosity. She wanted nothing of his style and his money anymore. Why should she? She had come and settled in England and worked hard and earned herself a respectable, reasonably paid position. There were good prospects and she lived in a nice flat. She wasn't ashamed to have her sister come to visit and she had a few pounds in the bank.

It was a solid, sensible life and, despite the boredom from time to time, she enjoyed it. But now, no matter what she felt, Paluzzi had decided he wanted her away from it. He wanted to take her from a secure world to a world of shadows.

Seated immobile on the bed, Serena decided bluntly that Paluzzi would have to be out-foxed. Fact was, she didn't *want* to go with him – and she didn't trust him. There was no fun in him anymore and there were too many question marks. She wouldn't go. But how could she refuse him?

For several moments she mulled that over, then an obvious answer came to her: she would have to tell the police about him. Not tomorrow, but *now*. That was the best answer. She was unsure of the address of the rented house, but she knew where the warehouse was. If she rang the police (what was that policeman's name he mentioned?) they could get him before the money was handed over. It would mean prison for him, but it would be freedom for her. And why should he suspect her of telling them? Surely, to him, she was a docile and obedient woman? But – better still – she could refract suspicion by claiming to be a girlfriend of one of this hit team – this Robertson, for example. Paluzzi was already wary of him, of all the team, so, if he heard he had been grassed on by one of them, he might easily believe it. There would be no reason to think of her as the informer.

The Dobermann Pinscher in the corner climbed out of its basket and ambled over to her. The rheumy red eyes stared up questioningly. One thing was certain, she felt. Her opportunity to defy Paluzzi was here and now. Come tomorrow, the chances would be gone.

She cuddled the dog up onto the bed and lay back to consider the risks.

'Turn left here and cut the lights,' Abney said, his voice clipped.

Bonney looked at the straggling lane ahead of them, silver and grey under moonlight, and quickly estimated that they were no more than ten miles from the zone north of Reading where, no doubt, the Squad's follow team would still be centering their search.

'Shut the bloody engine,' Abney rasped. 'It'll wake the dead.'

They were on a hill. Bonney threw the truck into neutral and allowed it to coast noiselessly down the slope. From the rise in the land he could see the few buildings dotted far apart down the lane. The nearest, a L-shaped brick affair with an enclosed yard, looked the most promising. Just as he saw it Abney spoke:

'Pull in under the pine trees. There's a picnic area there and you'll be covered from the road. I'll go on down to the warehouse and get the gear.' He hesitated, sitting with the cab door half-open. 'Maybe you'd better come. There's two cases.'

Bonney felt obliged to act the role. 'Will there be anyone down there? I mean, I don't want trouble.'

'You're *in*, mate. Full stop. Now, pull 'er in.'

The Scania hobbled up on the grass bank and edged in behind the neat rows of picnic tables. The creaking axles silenced and everything stilled. Abney threw open the door and jumped out. Bonney followed. They walked along in the speckled shade of the trees, not speaking. Away to their right the iridescent halo of the town's lights lit the sky like a sunset and, from that direction, riding on the wind came the muted buzz of traffic. Bonney motioned to speak loudly but Abney hushed him. Bonney asked again whether there was anybody in the warehouse. 'Doesn't look it, does it? I've no way of knowing. But the gear's in the back building, far as I know. Should be easy.'

Reaching the chicken-wire fence, they turned left and followed it, tramping round to the rear. Here, in the velvet shadows where no moonlight filtered down, they found the bolted double-door of the back entrance to the warehouse. Abney examined the lock with his fingers. 'Badly rusted,' he said. 'Light iron. Go and get a wheel-brace. I'll jemmy it.'

Running back to the truck Bonney considered the possibilities of trying to find a phone now. He could chance it, make back for town on foot. But it would take time, too much time. All right – he knew the location now, but he had Abney too, and he'd lost him once already and wasn't going to risk the encore.

Taking the jemmy, he ran back to Abney and handed it over. Five minutes of back-breaking levering sprung the bolt from the doors and they were in. Abney produced a small torch and its beam illuminated a wide vacant space with boxes stocked to their right. The first thing Bonney noticed after his quick look round was the smell in the warehouse – a rancid smell, almost of putrefaction. 'How many buildings are there?' Bonney asked.

'Just this and the old office,' Abney said. 'I don't think they connect. I've had a look round in daylight.'

'The stuff's here?' Bonney said. 'Where? In the crates?'

'Let's go through 'em.'

They crossed to the stacked boxes and Abney started examining the markings on them. Slowly, one by one, he checked each, grunting dissatisfaction every time. Moonlight twinkled in round the gaps at the front door and Bonney left Abney and casually tried the handles. With a steely whine the door gave inwards. Abney swivelled, hissed out of the dark. 'What're you doin'?'

'Just lookin'. Should I check the office building?'

Abney flicked the torch beam despondently over the boxes. Time was frittering away. If he wanted to get that boat.

'All right. But be very careful. There could be a fella there. You're looking for two crates, this high, with metal at the edges and foreign writing. Each has a red X on 'em too, top and sides.' He shut up quickly, sighed loud. 'I hope the bastard hasn't shifted 'em. Just my luck.' His eyes shone back towards Bonney. 'Easy does it.'

Bonney nodded and tip-toed out of the warehouse. In the open yard the brilliant light of the moon coloured the area like daylight. Two old tractors and a dark-painted Commer van were parked under an awning. Keeping in shadow of these, Bonney crossed to the doorway of the office building. It was locked with a standard Yale. Fumbling in his pockets Bonney found only the Scania keys. He took them out and measured them. The truck keys were useless but the finger of the RAC key on the ring looked slim and long enough. Slipping it between the lock and the wood jamb, he forced it down on the top of the iron tongue and wedged it back. The door swung open. The interior of the hallway looked forlorn, bleak.

If the place was empty and if there was a telephone, Bonney reflected, his luck would really be in. Moving gently, testing floorboards with his heel before setting weight on them, Bonney checked each of the four rooms on the lower floor. Two stood empty, clouded with cobwebs in the moon's rays. A third was a ramshackle mess with flooring removed and a million paint tins piled into corners. The fourth was locked. An alcove by the fourth floor gave onto a stairway. Bonney wasted no time and began to ascend. For a minute he stopped, thinking something in the murk at the top had moved – but this was an illusion framed by the dance of moonbeams through the skylight, he decided – and he walked on.

The first door he tried on the landing opened into a large office room and, with nothing stirring, he chanced turning on the light. The room yawned back at him – an ill-furnished square with drawn blinds and only a few office chairs. Remnants of a well-digested meal cluttered the desktop. Bonney's heart leapt. Bonanza! Hidden among brandy bottles, food wrappings and newspapers – a telephone.

He looked at his watch. One o'clock. The delay on the

farm track had cost them nearly an hour. Where would Hackett be now? Going south, to headquarters again? Or still combing the area? Either way, the call to the Yard would bring him back into play pretty fast. He stalled. Maybe he should wait till Abney definitely located the haul. What if it *had* been moved?

He took up the phone and dialled the cleared line to the Yard. It would be best to report the exact position, tell them to take up the tail immediately but give him breathing space unless he signalled them to swoop on the lorry. Perhaps Abney would direct him to another site.

The Yard line answered almost immediately. Before speaking he held the phone away from his ear and listened to the penetrating silence of the building. Comforted, he started talking.

'Lewis here. The Manifest request. Slight change. Don't pick us up yet because we haven't got it. My location is – '

An explosion of vibrant red burst through Bonney's head and he had a vague sensation the telephone leaping into the air and flailing across the room. Then blood rushed hotly down his nose and dripped into his throat. A searing pain knifed up his spine. Then, nothing . . . .

Down in the warehouse the dull boom of noise from outside made Abney jump in fright. On impulse he ducked down behind the crates and listened. What was it? Someone falling? Had there been a shout too? For some minutes he knelt in the dark, the sweat of his exertions, of pulling the Greek crates to the ground, rapidly drying in the cold. No more sound came. He stood up and switched on the torch, his thoughts preoccupied. That witless fool Lewis had probably fallen in the dark. A repeat performance of the lorry on the dirt-track. The boy was an incompetent, typical of the young-blood swells whom Dink often lovingly patronised. Suddenly, in the waving beam of the torch across the ground, something out of the ordinary took

Abney's eye. He straightened the beam and walked over. A red gelatinous substance was sparkling on the scrubbed concrete below a broken-down Ford tractor. As he came closer he saw the stalagmitical shape where the substance, now congealed, had dropped from the tractor cab. In stunned amazement he saw the bright red river marks of blood on the bodywork. Forgetting the importance of silence, he pulled the cab door open, oblivious to the scream of rotted hinges. When his hands reached in to the tarpaulin the first touch told him a body was lying there. Tearing the hard material out of the way, the glaring purple face of Gifford looked up at him. The overhead lights flashed on suddenly and a voice like a shotgun blast sounded behind him.

'Move and I'll blow your legs off!'

Abney froze. At the same time the clipped accent registered in his brain. A voice he was well familiar with. Ignoring the warning, he turned.

Robertson was standing just inside the door, his face strained in frenzy and the Walther Abney knew well in his hand. Crumpled in a heap at his feet lay Bonney.

No one spoke. Robertson's furious eyes moved quickly from Abney to the Greek crates, then back to the cab, to Gifford now sprawled half-out of the doorway. His face creased in shock and his mouth fell open. Abney, in turn, gaped from Robertson to the gun, then to the heaped body at his feet.

'You bastard,' Robertson said breathlessly. 'What d'you do to Giff?'

Abney turned back towards Gifford's body. He touched the face. It was icy cold.

'He's cold,' he muttered. 'I found him here. Who did it?'

Robertson kicked the bundle at his feet. 'You know him?'

'Yeah. A mate. You hit him? Is he okay?'

'A mate?' Robertson spat. 'What kind of a caper are you at? You've got the crates out? You dirty shit – are you selling out? Is that it? This guy was ringing someone, looking for a pick up.'

'What're you talking about? Who was he phoning?'

Still patently shocked by the scene, Robertson strolled into the warehouse and gingerly kicked the crates over. 'Bastard,' he repeated venomously. 'Doin' us all down. You scum. You're selling, are you?'

Abney stumbled forward and Robertson jerked the gun up. Abney pushed it out of the way in a friendly, cool gesture. 'Hold on,' he implored. 'There's some double-dealing here. Who killed Giff? You must've known he was here.'

Confused, Robertson crossed to the body and lifted the tarpaulin away. The mess of blood-soaked tissues spattered round the cab as he pulled off the brocade. 'He's been dead a while,' he mumbled. 'Someone dumped him.'

'Paluzzi maybe.' As Abney was speaking the words the realisation of the possible truth in them hit him with force. He stomped over to Robertson and pulled him away by the arm. 'That's it, you know. Old Giff wanted out. He went looking for the Italian. Jesus! That's what happened. I'll bet my life on it. The bum killed him. He wanted cash and the Italian did him in.'

Robertson's wide eyes stared, totally lifeless. 'He wouldn't . . . . Don't be stupid.'

'How else would the body get here?'

Robertson focussed on the comatose body in the doorway. 'What about you? That bastard. What's the trick?' His hand shot up and he grabbed Abney's lapel roughly. 'We're in this together.'

'It's a bummer. Giff had the right idea. He wanted out. The Crime Squad's onto Paluzzi. They want him. We'll swing with him.'

'So you're opting out? Takin' the gear and saying good-bye?'

'It's a dead-end with Paluzzi.' He shook Robertson's grip casually off. 'Look at Giff. Use your topper. Maybe that's what he's got planned for you next, eh? You never know. He's in a league by himself, that bastard.' Abney spat into his hands and began trying to scrub off the thick blood stains. 'I never said I trusted that shit. My thinking is, it's best to outdo him while you can.'

'You're outdoin' us all though, aren't you?'

Abney shrugged. 'C'mon with me. I've a deal lined up. Just as good as you'll get.'

'And who's that kid?' Robertson tossed his head towards Bonney. Abney shrugged thoughtfully, strolled over and crouched beside him. He began rifling the pockets. 'You said he was trying to ring someone? I don't get it. Unless –' He stood up quickly. 'I could've been planted.' His body had become rigid and he stood staring down at Bonney with a crazed expression. 'Jesus,' he hissed. 'I'll kill that whore – '

'Who is he?'

'Driver. I wanted to get the gear to Ireland.' Abney suddenly became animated. He began ranting vehemently. 'Look, this could be a corner. This gaff'll be blown. I want to move this gear – we've got to. I have a lorry up the road. We'll leave it. What transport have you? I've a mate in Bristol. Down the M4, no trouble. We can move it, get it to Dublin later.'

Robertson's eyes, like his thoughts, were racing – from Gifford, to Bonney, to the crates. 'Can't be a police corner – why would he ring up?'

'Bugger him. Chance I'm not taking! I'm moving.'

'Not with the gear, you're not.'

Abney grew red-faced. 'For Christ's sake, you bloody fool. Look what's been done to Giff. Explain it. That's

Paluzzi – you said it yourself not too long ago – he'd strangle his own mother!'

'All right,' Robertson shouted. 'Could've been – Giff could've asked for it. We don't know. But there's more than you – there's the team. No one's coppin' out on them. *I* say so. Now the swap is already going. Paluzzi has the first call in.'

'He can put it up his arse, mate. I'm taking the gear. If I were you I'd put a match to this kip and scarper.' He jabbed a finger at Bonney. 'That kid's mean shit from somewhere.'

'He's yours,' Robertson snapped. 'If he's messy, you brought 'im – remember that.'

Angrily turning away from Abney, Robertson began lifting the Greek crates, hauling them back up on the stacked boxes. The gun, Abney saw, was in his waistband. Both hands were occupied. With ten seconds to decide, Abney launched forward, jumped for the jemmy from the Scania and lunged at Robertson. The first blow solidly connected with Robertson's cheek bone and a gash of nine inches sprouted across the side of his face. Still on balance, he dropped the Greek crate and kicked out at Abney, but the blow was badly judged. His boot sank under Abney's arm. Abney lashed down with the jemmy, contacting with force on Robertson's forehead. Like a pole-axed ox, Robertson slumped to the ground.

Over at the door Bonney had stirred into consciousness and lay prostrate, trying to remember where he was, trying to unravel the significance of what was being said around him. With agonising effort he twitched and rolled over on his back. A blurred image towered above him – a man, a handsome man with chubby jowls. The man was leaning over him. The eyes looked alert, concerned. Bonney opened his mouth to talk, to ask for help. The man lifted his arms quickly, as if a crazy puppeteer had tugged at strings.

Something glistened in the overhead light. The man was swinging something. At the last moment Bonney realised it was a steel jemmy the man brandished.

The blow smashed down on Bonney's head and he plummeted into depthless space.

10

Area Six, one of several prearranged locations chosen by Hackett as possible bases from which to conduct the ransom swap, comprised a large disused military airfield with a derelict hanger and some out-houses, bordered on all sides by rich farmland and situated on the southern edge of the Hampshire Downs. Fortuitously, its position was not five miles from the nominated Andover exchange spot.

When Hackett and Louise arrived not long after one, the first cars were already there, the generator was rattling away and informally dressed men and women scurried around looking, Louise noted, blasé and morose. Night fever, she surmised.

Inside the brick building behind the hanger which apparently deemed itself 'headquarters', limpet lights had been rigged and an ancient, doorless solid-fuel stove had been lit. Four Crime Squad men and one girl hovered round this like moths at a light. The conversation was desultory. A portable UHF on the ground beside the stove relayed curt messages, calling various units, asking positions, advising movements. Hackett strode into this broad room, speaking loud, rocking the church tone of chatter. 'Right – ransom car – where?'

'Coming up,' a jaded-faced inspector replied, consulting a clip-board list. 'Lennie's in it, and some cash. Should be here any minute. And the 'copter. Bit of a job shaking the pilot out of bed, I should imagine.'

'We pay 'em well enough,' Hackett quipped dully. He joined the girl officer unfurling a map and pinning it to the wood-faced brick. With adept speed she placed it, marked it, then retreated. For a few silent minutes Hackett studied it, calculating distances on a biro's edge, marking possible car placings. Before he had finished Lennie arrived, lively and keen. The money was in the 1800 in the hanger. A couple of hundred thousand, most of it micro-filmed – and in the leather cases required. Hackett was ordering Lennie to band the whole squad together for a briefing when the powerful roar of the approaching helicopter shut him up. Lennie mimed his intentions and ran off.

Hackett and Louise walked outside, muffling themselves against the freezing breeze that rolled off the hills. The moon was high, climbing through ghostly pools of noctilucent clouds, and the stars shone with diamond-blue light. From their plateau post there were excellent views on three sides across the surrounding land and it pulsated with life, Louise thought fancifully, in contrast with the motionless heavens. Below them, lights bubbled gaily, wind sighed through foliage and car horns hooted a million miles away, crying like geckos in swamps. Louise and Hackett stood closely side-by-side, the wind stinging their eyes till tears came, watching the massive hulk of the Bell Jet Ranger 'copter swooping in over the plains. To both of them, there was something incredibly grotesque about the scene – this infinite gentleness of night obliterated by the angry scream of a monster machine. With ugly ease the 'copter drew over the flat space in front of the hanger, paused briefly, then began a slow, ear-shattering descent. Louise turned away. At last the wheels crunched down and the blades spun slower. The door opened and two men skipped out. One, Hackett knew as the ex-serviceman pilot who leased his civilian club's facilities to the Regional Crime Squad; the other was Price, an ace member of the squad.

Quickly greeting them Hackett marshalled them into the brick 'command' hut and, without preamble, launched into a fast account of the situation facing them. There were twenty-eight personnel present – when all arrived there would be thirty-two. These would be distributed through fifteen cars spread around all roads into Andover. Lennie, a one-time test driver at Silverstone, would handle the swap car. The instruction was to go to a children's playground, but, Hackett felt, this would be just one in a chain of 'contact' sites. A good, fast driver was needed to pace the operation. The helicopter was a useful stand-by and, though the difficulties of using it at night were clear, it could be brought into play for long-distance emergency look-outs since the moon was full and visibility was superb. On top of that, the likelihood was that the paper-chase could go on till dawn or later. There was no knowing when exactly the villains would try to collect the cash. It was imperative that the follows should be executed at low profile. Any overt moves might scare the collector off and the longer the business went on, the harder it would get. Hackett felt optimistic, he said, that if clean contact was eventually made and the loot taken, the inevitable cut-out line – the handing of cash from one to another – could be chased down and the final source – Paluzzi – could be got to. There was a hurried question session then. Some of the junior men wanted to know what kind of pick-up vehicles Hackett anticipated. Hackett admitted he could only guess at it. There were marked disadvantages about a swap in the middle of the night, but there were bonuses too. A small car – even a motorcycle – could find a country road, switch off lights and slip out of a net fairly easily; there would be less traffic hold-ups.

Someone else asked about Bonney's run. Hackett explained that no message had been received but that that fact could be interpreted in many ways; personally he felt it would be best to exclude Bonney from considerations of the job ahead. If luck was with him and things had gone well, it was probable that the stock house for the haul was already known. But a hundred and one intervening circumstances might have arisen. The safest thing to do would be play the job as an all-in swap and follow; hope for outside breaks – but don't rely on them.

As the last squad teams arrived Hackett directed them one by one to the various holding points ringed round the town. Just as the meeting broke he addressed everyone with a last grim speech.

'Not necessary to say we *have to* get that bronze gear back. It's priceless in every sense and it was lifted in our back garden. But we've a fight with Paluzzi, the big boy, too. Whatever happens tonight, we need Paluzzi. We've got to follow the line and hope for him. Be sure of what you do. Don't take risks. We have Paluzzi for murder, or conspiracy to commit, we have him for the haul. We must get him – right?'

Shortly before half-one the fleet of cars dashed off the airfield, bound for the town, and Lennie set off in the 1800, trailed by Hackett and Louise in the Capri. Motoring towards the town a dress rehearsal UHF check was initiated, each car calling its successor on a numbered basis. The Jet Ranger went airborne for a few minutes and, acting as a low-flying satellite, it joined the network, quickly giving short information of the small traffic movements on the main roads to the town. Then it touched down again, awaiting Hackett's advice on further movements.

In a matter of ten minutes Lennie and Hackett had reached the children's playground. As Lennie turned into the gravel park in front of it, Hackett drove slowly past, closely watching the situation. The playground was hemmed in on three sides by high buildings. The building to its left was a cinema and it was in the expansive car park of this that Lennie was stopping now.

Hackett pushed on for a half-mile, then pulled into a

cul-de-sac and turned the car. 'There was a phone box beside the playground,' Louise said. Hackett nodded. Contact would almost certainly be made via that. The UHF sang. 'Hackett? Five. I'm in the church lane. Can see Lennie here. AOK.'

'Report moves.'

'Yeah.'

They waited. Louise sat geared uncomfortably forward in her seat, her lips pursed anxiously. Hackett listened to his own breathing. The cold was intense. 'I wonder is Paluzzi listening in,' Louise said, eyeing the radio. Hackett frowned. 'Too troublesome. He wouldn't need to, knows he'd just get jumbles. No. This affair is easier for him than you'd think.'

Silence again. Louise slid her hand under her blouse to feel the heat of her belly. Hackett blew into cupped hands.

The UHF again: 'Five. Lennie's moving. Leaving 1800. Phone box. Must be ringing.'

'Watch the car,' Hackett snapped.

Again they waited in hushed expectancy. The minutes edged by. Again the UHF roused them, this time the echoing voice was Lennie's. 'Hackett? Get that? Phone call – just said, hold on for contact.'

'Keep off the blower!' Hackett snapped. 'Look clean.'

'What does that mean – wait for contact?' Louise said airily. 'Someone going to collect here?'

'I wouldn't have bet on it,' Hackett said, an unhappy scowl contorting his features. 'Bit odd.' He shrugged. 'Maybe there's a delay on Paluzzi's end.'

Price's voice came over the radio. 'All standing by. Lennie's staying put. What do we do?'

'Cross your pins and wait,' Hackett answered grimly.

Louise felt seeds of depression blossoming in her mind. Given Paluzzi's history, given the fact of no contact from Bonney, given the reputation of the Five, she felt suddenly that no actuary worth his salt would assess the chances of a neat wrap-up at more than a thousand to one against. She looked into Hackett's face for reassurance but saw only a hollow, haggard mask.

Paluzzi put down the telephone and stared at it with perplexed eyes. What was wrong? Why wasn't Robertson answering? He had arranged to call at one but his repeated efforts met with just the non-ending purr of an engaged line. What had happened? Had Robertson accidentally left the receiver off the hook? Was there a problem with the line?

He stood up and pulled his topcoat on. He had no choice – he would have to go to the warehouse. He must have confirmation that the cut-outs were in operation, otherwise leading the money on to the chosen hand-over spot in Savernake Forest made no sense. He had intended to avoid all further contact with the warehouse, but that couldn't be helped now. Anyway, he was only five minutes by car away from the place, so the short delay could easily be shouldered.

Driving fast from the detached bungalow only recently rented by him, Paluzzi kept to the back roads and made the warehouse in good time. Approaching from the opposite direction to Bonney's arrival route he parked again in the heavy copse a little away from the buildings and went the rest of the way on foot. Before opening the gate he looked cautiously into the yard. In the light of the moon the Volvo was visible, and the black shape of the other tractor, and the warehouse door appeared securely locked. Everything seemed in order. Paluzzi took out his keys and lifted the padlock. The lock swung free in his hands and the gate rolled open. Immediately his senses quickened. He opened his topcoat and the single button of the mohair suit beneath, giving access to the Luger in a triple-draw holster at his waistband. An ephemeral image of this faceless man called Hackett flashed swiftly into his mind. A sixth sense told him that kind of threat was near to hand. He thought about going back, but walked on. Then he saw the light under the warehouse door. Drawing the Luger he shinned forward, stooping deftly to his knees and flinging the door in. The hairs on the nape of his neck bristled frighteningly. He shuddered.

There was blood everywhere.

Gifford's body, spreadeagled like a half-dismembered doll, lay below the old cab. Clotted heaps of blood were splashed around it, glowing black on the bleached concrete ground. Across from him, lying face up, his mouth working noiselessly, breathing through bubbles of blood, lay Robertson. Not far from where he lay another body – a bearded young man with blood-matted brown hair – crouched, half-sitting, half-lying. Paluzzi's head shot up and he glanced across the ground. There were little lakes of liquid all over the place, rainbow-coloured, the unmistakable hue of petrol. Across at the rear doors someone had tried to light a fire. A huge scorched lick, from ground to roof, was notched into the wood. Robertson was beginning to moan now, disconnected words gurgling through blood. Paluzzi slipped the safety catch back on his gun and ran over to the heaped boxes. The recognition of what had happened hit him like a pile-driver in the gut. He stopped dead. *The crates!* The crates were gone. Somebody had taken them. A hand, Robertson's hand, touched his shoe and he jumped. The moaning was loud now and the broken eyes were staring up. Paluzzi leant down. 'What happened? Who was it?' His own voice was almost unintelligible.

'. . . Abney . . . took . . . trick . . . .'

'The Bronze Boy?' Paluzzi croaked. 'He took it? Where? When?'

As he spoke he took out a handkerchief and mopped the blood away from Robertson's lips. There were three enormous fissures across the cranium and face, he saw, but it would be impossible to judge how serious the damage was. 'To Bristol,' Robertson stammered. 'He took van . . . headed Bristol . . . motorway . . . .'

'You're sure?'

The lips moved but no words came out. Paluzzi shook the big shoulders softly. 'C'mon. You sure it's Bristol? How long's he gone?'

'Bristol . . . not long . . . . Get doctor . . . .'

Paluzzi dropped Robertson's limp body and moved over to Bonney. The skull wounds looked less severe but the man had taken a nasty blow on the forehead. Paluzzi knelt to him and tried to revive him but thumping the chest and rough shaking achieved nothing. He dropped him. Who was he? he wondered quickly. A cut-out? One of Robertson's bumbling cronies? Most likely.

He crossed to the door. Both men were probably critically ill, but there was nothing he could do for them. They were on Abney's conscience, not his, he thought lightly. He ran out into the night. The mission would have to abort. He could do nothing without go-betweens and forcing a ransom without the goods could be deadly. He would have to catch Abney. How much of a head start would he have? An hour, an hour-and-a-half? Certainly no more, and in the old Commer van he wouldn't have gone too far. The Mercedes would catch him.

Jumping into the car he raced up through the gears and found the road signposted to the motorway. Memories of his last job in Britain came to him – of the abandoned arms run and the brutal fight with the Crime Squad at the docks. He had been sure of that job once upon a time; but it let him down.

For the first time in all his weeks of planning the possibility of utter defeat touched his thoughts.

Twenty minutes that felt like twenty hours had passed and Hackett and Louise still sat in the enervating cold of the Capri. The UHF beat on heartlessly, like the voice of a mocking demon. Lennie was still in the cinema car park. All cars were still in position. No further contact had been made by the villains. There was no news of Bonney or the loaned truck. Something was definitely wrong. All patrols on motorways and in the Midlands and South had been alerted to watch for the truck but not one report had come in.

'There's a hitch on the ransom,' Hackett said at last. 'No doubt 'bout it. This isn't form. Maybe Bonney and Abney have blown it.' Louise looked at his profile, saw nothing but tiredness.

'What do we do?' she said.

'Mobilise. Everyone out for the truck. Hope.'

Hackett took up the radio and was about to speak when his name was called roughly over the air. The bad-textured line suggested the transceiver at Area Six command. He acknowledged, his grip tightening fiercely on the hand mike. The urgency in the call had been noticed by Louise too. Now she slunk imperceptibly closer to the receiver, her eyes wide.

'Hackett? Call received HQ. Tip-off. Italian's location north of Newbury. Wallin Lane. Transport Company named 'Whiteline'. Repeat – '

Louise heard Hackett stutter and choke on words for the first time in their working life. Ascertaining that the call had been made to the Crime Squad base and the caller had claimed to be a girlfriend of James Robertson's, he instantly turned the ignition and sped off. Ordering nine cars to maintain cover on the playground just in case, he called the other five to join him and instructed the 'copter to go airborne and head towards Newbury. In order to avoid startling anyone prematurely he told the pilot to take her up to fifteen or sixteen thousand feet and circle west of the town.

There was no traffic on the roads now and within seconds almost some of the other squad cars had caught up with him and were beating a fast route north. There was a short delay while they searched the northern edge of the town looking for the lane. Then one of the cars found it, radioed the rest and, like birds of prey, the five swooped on the small road, barring both ends of it and scanning the terrain. Hackett sat in the front rank position, parked on top of the hill that looked across the buildings and hedges that lined the road.

The terse, non-stop cross-talk that hammered out of the UHF fogged his thoughts and he lowered the volume. There was only one road, no side-paths, nothing. Visibility under the moon was excellent. Of the buildings along the road the nearest, the L-shaped enclosure, looked the most likely. It was difficult to make out detail at this distance, but the place was in darkness and looked to be innocuously in slumber. Hackett clicked on the UHF and asked two of the men from a car at the other end of the road to advance, on foot, and meet him at the chicken wire fence. Then, slipping out into the whistling breeze with Louise taking the Capri's wheel, he ran down the hill in shelter of the high bushes, waving like black fountains against the sky. He had been carrying the Smith & Wesson since the State Visit alert and now, with the automatic timing of a pro soldier nearing battle, he undid his jacket and clasped the butt with his right hand. The building, he could see now, was clearly a small office block with a warehouse attached. Was this the warehouse Abney spoke of? Was this the hoarding spot and Paluzzi's operations base? . . . An almost incoherent welter of questions coursed through his head. Undoubtedly the tip had come from an informed source, taking the Robertson reference into account. But who? Momentarily he considered Dink. Had she known more than she'd said? He shrugged that off. If there had been any other way for her, he guessed, she would not have given up Abney.

Coming out into a clearance in the bushes Hackett faltered in his step and stopped. The loaned truck – the instantly recognisable Scania with its green-covered Dennison Tilt that Bonney had chosen – sat like a stranded monster whale deep in the pines. Gun drawn, Hackett carefully checked the cab and looked through the canvas. Everything was silent and lifeless. He moved on, his thoughts more confused than ever. Was it possible that Bonney and Abney had taken all this time to get here and had not yet lifted the goods? Had Bonney been blown? Was he, and Paluzzi, and the rest of them, in there?

Reaching the wire fence he crouched down and waited. Footfalls scrunched the grass and two Squad men dived down beside him. '"Whiteline"', one of the men reported. 'Front gate open. No lights. Two tractor cabs in yard.'

'Let's try the back,' Hackett said. One of the other squad men was armed and Hackett saw a flame of moonlight on a barrel of steel and heard the safety catch being released. 'Easy does it,' he whispered and the cool eyes shifted to him and confirmed.

They came to the rear double-door of the warehouse and saw the blackened marks of a small fire. Hackett touched the wood and it flaked crisply. The pitted surface was warm to the touch. He leant to the bolt that held the door and with no more than a nimble prod, the doors swung open. An animal sound of agony, waxing and waning, came from within. 'Torch?' Hackett nudged the armed man. A light beam jumped on and the warehouse interior became visible. Deflected light skimmed off a confetti of blood and petrol patches. The men walked quietly in. The beam picked out two bodies, one quite dead, the other seemingly not far from. 'Old Gifford,' Hackett said stonily. He knelt beside Robertson and rubbed the blood from his eyes with his bare fingers. 'And Mr Organisation himself.' He lay Robertson flat on the ground. The breathing was shallow and weak and already the man had lost maybe two pints of blood. As Hackett went to stand up, ordering one of the squad men to look for light switches, the door through which they had entered rattled on its hinges and a tottering voice from the shadows said, 'Jesus, you took a long time comin'.'

The overhead lights shot on and Bonney half-stood, back propped against the double-door. His knees looked shaky and cascades of blood rippled down from his forehead. Hackett dashed to him just as his balance shifted and he toppled down. A harmless-looking lath obviously intended for defence clattered to the ground from his hand. 'Check over the rest of the place,' Hackett shouted to the squad men and they hurried out to the enclosed yard. ''S all right,' Bonney said strongly. 'They're gone. No one about. Abney quit with the merchandise, far as I know.' He lifted a hand and brushed dribbles of blood from his eyelashes. 'Didn't get the whole story, but he's gone to somewhere in Bristol, an old friend's. I heard him say the M4 – '

'You sure? Long gone?'

Bonney shook his head jerkily. 'Three-quarters of an hour, more. Don't remember much – ' He smiled hideously, his teeth rimmed with blood. 'Paluzzi came too. No mistaking. Slick dick. Not twenty minutes. Lugged me round a bit but I lay doggo. Think he's gone after the goods.'

Defeat and depression sloughed off Hackett like the skin of a snake. He grinned. 'What were they driving? C'mon you happy bastard – what can you tell?' A distant metallic whirr, the sound of the Jet Ranger at high altitude, made both of them gear up excitedly. Bonney said, 'Dunno what cars there were. Abney wanted to leave the truck – I heard him say it. There was a grey Commer van in the yard and two tractors.'

'I'll check it.' Hackett said. 'What about Paluzzi? C'mon, kiddo. Think.'

Bonney shook his head gingerly. 'Saw nothing. I was flying. Heard him rough Robertson – that's it. He charged off.'

Hackett pulled Bonney up and sat him on a fallen crate. Blood was beginning to clot and dry on his forehead and he offered to come with Hackett, but when he tried to walk his legs buckled like reeds in wind. Calling one of the squad men to look after Bonney and get ambulances in, Hackett ran into the yard and under the awning. A Volvo and Scania were still there but there was a naked opening where, clearly, a van-sized vehicle had been parked.

He ran.

The ribbon of road stretched before him, totally empty. The trees had stopped swaying and even the breeze seemed to have died. The cold was gone and hot sweat lathered his back. The moon, like the prize at the end of the race, glittered magnificently at the top of the hill. The pump of his heart was in his throat. His mind closed. It was all a childhood game. It was him or them. They were well matched, but he could be better if he tried. If he ran faster, faster. Lengthening his stride he started on the hill, the sciatic nerve in his back screaming with the strain, his chest tightening.

By the time the Crime Squad cars came into sight Paluzzi had forced himself back into his mind, but he felt jubilant. The question marks were gone and the course had been narrowed. All that remained now were the clinical factors of speed and time. If he could make up that time

Abney had gained; if he could get to Abney before Paluzzi did; if he could lure Paluzzi into the trap of Abney's van and the treasure . . . .

Gaining the Capri at last he whipped up the UHF and gasped out two blunt demands: to Area Six command he ordered that Divisional police should be requested to prepare road-blocking for all M4 junctions from Newbury to Bristol, but to await instructions about the vehicles wanted. Then he called the Jet Ranger, asking it to fly north to the motorway and pick him and three other men up.

Louise asked no questions. She started the car in a hurry.

The Merc hit a hundred and fifteen and flattened off. Paluzzi held his foot down on the boards and watched only the snow-coloured road directly in front of the bonnet, scarred and ugly with the graffiti of a thousand skid-marks. At three minute intervals, like an automaton, he glanced up from the roadway and eyed the distant prospect, looking for signs of the Commer. He knew now he was close to it. The old van would do no more than forty-five, and there had been a considerable delay outside Swindon, east of Junction 15, where one of the big AEC Diesels had overturned and all but one lane of the motorway was closed. He had been stalled there too, but, unlike the Commer, he had been quickly able to make up for the loss of time. The night traffic was light – mostly the expected juggernauts playing their inter-city trades – and the Merc was singing like a bird and a bomb.

The thought paramount among Paluzzi's thoughts was whether or not he would kill Abney. The annoyance at the failure of his night-swap plans had quickly subsided, and he was in no doubt that the Bronze Boy and other treasures could be easily redeemed. But in a warped, perverse way he found himself admiring the style of this man Abney, despite the perfidy. It was men such as these he needed in Britain – clever, self-advancing men who would be ruthless but painstakingly careful in getting what they wanted. He had never met Abney, and he was sorry now that he would be seeing him for the first time in pitched warfare. Had he not used that fool Robertson....? He shut his mind. The deal had blown and Abney, as a traitor, would have to die. An entirely new plan would have to be designed and he would need new help, new associates. He would go abroad again, maybe smuggle the treasures with him. The British, he thought sourly, fought too hard to make competition worthwhile.

Breasting a hill on the motorway, the twin lights of a boxy van ahead came into view. Paluzzi angled forward. The speedometer needle quivered either side of one-twenty and he started gaining fast. He looked in the rearview mirror and saw no lights behind. Ahead too everything looked clear. Conditions were ideal. A turn-off to Chippenham lay ahead, to the left. No waiting, he must hit fast.

As he drew close he saw, quite unmistakably, that the Commer van was the same one he had seen in the yard. The rear mudguards were painted a light grey and it sported double number plates. He braked hard as the Merc slid past it and held a line parallel for a moment. Sure enough, one man sat at the wheel – a big fellow with crew-cut hair and a fat face. From old photographs in newspapers he recognised him. This was Abney all right, no doubt about it. Paluzzi took out his Luger and pulled the car back in speed, trailing behind the van. Stretching over, he lowered the window of the passenger door. Icy, wet wind shot in, stunning him. The Merc swerved into a wavering circle, swung back out and corrected itself. Abney was driving in the slow lane. Paluzzi moved the Merc fifteen yards away into the fast overtaking lane. Again he accelerated level with the van. He looked at the speedometer and saw they were cruising at forty-eight. Abney's face turned casually towards him, glanced at the Merc and along the length of it, then turned back to the road. Unwary. Stupid man.

Paluzzi took the gun in his left hand, held the steering wheel with the right and aimed out the open window at the van. He fired twice. The first shot connected. The van shuddered and wobbled out into the middle of the road. Paluzzi had a momentary impression of Abney reacting in fright, swinging round to look towards the rear. It didn't dawn on him to look towards the Merc. The back tyre had punctured beautifully and great slivers of rubber were peeling rapidly off, spinning round the wheel like dead snakes. The double exhaust of the van boomed as Abney tore down in gear and aimed the nose in to the hard shoulder. Paluzzi, having driven past as if naturally overtaking, tooted his horn twice in polite acknowledgement and pulled in too. He stopped the car thirty yards from Abney's van, then reversed slowly to within inches of the front grille. Abney was already out, examining the remains of his tyre. Gripping the Luger tightly in his side coat pocket, Paluzzi alighted and sauntered back. Abney glanced indifferently up. 'Blow out,' he said. 'Pretty bad considering speed.' He didn't recognise the pleasant-faced man in the good-quality clothes, took him for a businessman, a doctor maybe. Paluzzi smilingly leant down beside him, as if to inspect the wheel. Abney stiffened, grunted. Something hard was thrust into his ribs. Paluzzi said, 'Help me put the Greek stuff into the Mercedes, Abney.' There was nothing hysterical or urgent in the tone. Abney couldn't speak and Paluzzi hoisted him to his feet. The surprise – the devastating shock of having come so far so easily then finding this nameless stranger standing between a fortune and nothing – rendered Abney dumb and immobile. At first, crazily, he thought the man was police, then the pieces of puzzle slotted into place. The brown face, the prinker's get-up, the flat accent. This, for the first time, was Frank Paluzzi, the top man himself.

When Abney didn't speak Paluzzi said, 'Get the keys, open the rear.'

Dumbly, Abney gave way. He walked to the driver's door and opened it. Paluzzi was yards away, standing near the back of the van. Abney halted. Robertson's Walther was lying on the passenger's seat. 'Hurry up,' Paluzzi said. 'It's cold.' Abney said nothing. He took up the Walther and slipped the clip. Stuffing it into his zip-up leather jacket, he ambled back to Paluzzi proffering the keys. Paluzzi backed away from him. 'You do it,' he said, moving further away as if making sure there was no trap to be sprung from the back of the van.

Abney conceded, opened the doors and pulled the Bronze Boy crate out onto the macadam. As he did, in a smooth agile dive, he sank behind the crate, drew the Walther and fired. Totally unprepared, Paluzzi jumped in fright, side-stepping a fraction, and the bullet sizzled past his ear lobe. Quickly regaining himself he rolled to the ground, spun over till his body dropped into a shallow ditch and extended his gun hand. As he was about to pull the trigger a buzzing roar checked him. Abney fired again but the shot went wildly astray. Paluzzi turned on his back in the rye grass. He glanced up the motorway. No cars approached, but the ear-piercing drone grew louder, nearer. Instinctively he looked to the sky. It might have sounded perhaps like a monoplane, or something even larger, but no warning lights were visible in the clear sky. Arching up to look around again, Abney fired a third time and the bullet plucked at the elbow of his coat and rent it, drawing small blood. A sting of pain shook him.

Above in the Jet Ranger rushing over the motorway at hearly a hundred knots with all lights out, both Hackett and the pilot simultaneously saw the parked vehicles and the beacon of flame as the Walther shot. 'Stall 'er!' Hackett screamed. 'Down, down!' He took the radio and relayed a swift message to all units, informing his exact position and instructing patrols to close the roads immediately.

The 'copter slewed over the Merc, curled left and paused, a hundred feet up. Hackett stared down, the three men in the back crowding the windows to see what action was in progress. They saw nothing. One car. A van. No more. There appeared to be a crate lying close to the rear of the van, its metal fittings shining in the moon. The pilot flicked on powerful spotlights and tilted, yawing left then right to comb the immediate area of the vehicles. For a minute no one came into sight. Then a man appeared to crawl from under the van, scurry forward, grab the crate and run to the Merc.

'Down!' Hackett shouted, drawing his Smith & Wesson.

The 'copter sank fast. Hackett had the door open before they were fifty feet from the ground. Everyone peered back. The escaping man was getting into the Merc, dumping the crate in the back. Now the car was starting to move, lurching uncertainly forward as if the driver was unfamiliar with it. Hackett gestured the pilot to go lower. The 'copter dropped, positioned broadside-on across the road a hundred yards ahead of the Merc. 'More!' Hackett yelled. It was down to about twenty feet now, the thunder of the rotor blades rebounding off the ground. The Merc was accelerating towards it. Hackett forced the door open further and prepared to shoot. The Merc darted left at the wrong moment. Pitching backwards and down for safer positioning, the Jet Ranger swooped very near to the ground, just on the hard shoulder. The Merc, trying to race through the gears, crossed onto the shoulder, tried to swerve to avoid, but crashed directly into the wheels and underbelly. For a second Hackett thought the 'copter was down. The gnarring tear as metal and glass splintered shuddered up through the seats and through their bodies. Hackett heard his gun crack onto the floor and saw the world turn on its side. One of the men in the back let out a half-scream of shock and terror. But the pilot's reflexes saved them. Pulling back the joy-stick and opening the throttle, he jolted the craft upwards as fast as he could, backing it away from the smash area. Just as he did they saw the Merc slide slowly forward, its top half almost flattened to bonnet level, jaunt across the road and ram into the crash-barrier of the fast lane. As it crashed, flames shot out, twisting from under the engine, licking at the passenger door. Hackett mimed to the pilot to take the 'copter down again and, though the underbelly and wheels were badly twisted, making a proper touch-down impossible, the pilot eased down to within a few feet of the ground and Hackett and the squad men leapt out.

They headed immediately for the treasure. Tongues of searing flame were engulfing the front of the car now and the likelihood of explosion was obvious. Hackett chanced it, trotting forward, tearing open the rear door and dragging the crate out as one might a dying man. Briefly, before he started to run, he looked across to the mutilated man behind the wheel. In death Stan Abney looked serene and sullen. Pathetic, Hackett thought crazily, because it had all only been a twirl on the roundabout for him and he'd paid the ultimate price for miscuing the players and the game.

Hackett had just managed to pull the crate fifty yards from the Merc when the fire found the feed petrol pipes and ran to the tank. With savage fury the car exploded, vast chunks of tortured metal flinging high into the placid sky. Then the big flames took over, buffeting and howling in the turgid breeze.

As the squad men stood gaping at the inferno, protectively shading the Greek crate, Hackett turned back to the Commer and looked inside. Paluzzi hadn't been far from his thoughts since the Merc and van first came into view. He had guessed Abney and the Italian had fought it out and one or the other of them was preparing escape with the treasures when the 'copter arrived. The flicker of the gun-shot had made him think one of them had been killed, and somehow his money was on Paluzzi to stay alive. Then the Merc had crashed and he had assumed he'd find the shattered body of Paluzzi there. But no. Paluzzi, as ever, was not to be seen.

The treasure was intact – two crates marked in the precise way Hackett had been informed. The Commer van was Abney's getaway vehicle; and the Merc was then Paluzzi's. But there was no Paluzzi.

Hackett strode out into the road and looked down the long vista of emptiness. Blue lights twinkled in the far distance – police patrols blocking the road, no doubt. He looked to the land each side of the motorway. Flat, featureless fields. Nothing more. No barns, no houses, no hiding-places. The moon had begun its descent but visibility was still very good. And the Jet Ranger was still hovering around at about five hundred feet, occasionally dropping, its sharp remaining spotlight – the undamaged one – throwing a good area into almost day-time light. When the spotlight found him he threw out his arms and made wide signals, instructing the pilot to bring some Squad cars on to the scene. The pilot acknowledged by switching the spot on and off, then climbing high, perhaps to increase its radio range. Hackett turned to look after it as it edged down the motorway, its light drifting from side to side. Then he saw him. His eyes narrowed and he shook his head. The image was gone. He looked again. For an instant he had thought there was a man bundled low, creeping through the long grass at the road's edge. Now, when the 'copter's light washed back over the area, not a hundred yards away, the man was gone.

Hackett started walking down the road.

Suddenly, like a hunted animal, the figure in the distance shot up above the grass, swivelled towards Hackett, then turned and began running desperately. Hackett froze, his hand on his gun. He sucked in air and went to shout, to call for help but a pounding in his head stopped him. It had been just like this six years ago. At the docks. That insane night. Paluzzi and the squad. Everything had looked straightforward. Just a question of arresting villains. Then at the last minute they'd realised he had side-stepped them and they'd had to run to another location to try to take him. Hackett had arrived first at the wharf that night. He had fired first. And Paluzzi and his tough boys had fired back, a blaze of horror shooting. Something in Hackett's nerve had snapped that night – it had never happened before or since – but the shooting had rocked him, scared him. One way or the other they were outclassed by the sheer ruthlessness of Paluzzi's tactics, but Hackett had taken his two men and settled into a cast-iron safe cover spot. He might have held that point and waited till the fight expired in the inevitable course with no more ammo to hand, but he had used his pocket radio instead and called in support. The support that came wasn't a well-equipped bloody army – it was three unarmed men, one a good mate of Hackett's, the Super in charge of operations. The men had wallowed in at his call and each been mown down by the sten in Paluzzi's hands. Hackett had witnessed it all, and tried to save them but the surge of courage and effort had come too late. Clinically analysed, it had been one of those gremlins that materialise in the record books as 'miscalculations', instances the like of which he had seen on countless occasions among senior and junior men over the years. But the penalty for that miscalculation had been high, too high and the onus, even if only in his mind, rested *fully* with him for calling those men in. He had regretted the events of that night for six whole years, often reliving them painfully. All along he had hoped for the opportunity of a return bout. The chance to re-do the job, and do it properly. To get revenge too maybe.

And here, with the Greek hit, was the replay.

For a full three minutes Hackett watched Paluzzi scramble, running away through the brambles and grass of the roadside ditch. Then, very slowly, he started running after him. Two hundred yards on Paluzzi climbed across the wooden fence that bordered the road and ran into a grazing field. Hackett speeded up. He vaulted the fence and started sprinting. For his age and heavy build, Paluzzi made remarkably good headway. Keeping a long lead on Hackett he ran over the crest of a hillock and disappeared. Hackett put on the speed and charged to the high ground. At the top he stopped to catch his breath.

The terrain at the other side of the hill was more cluttered, less open. To his left a series of shambly sheds that looked like one-time stables ran in a broken line towards a roofless old farmhouse. Beech hedges crowded the ground to his right and ahead, a mile away, were the fairy lights of a village. Every cell of Hackett's rational brain told him to turn round and shout for cover and help, but the memories intruded, goaded him. He walked forward, sensing Paluzzi was near – in hiding perhaps, watching him, taking aim.

An owl hooted and far away a train echoed its call.

Hackett edged across to the beech hedges and stood close to them, listening. His palms were damp and he rubbed them roughly down the sides of his trousers. It was impossible to believe the case had come to this: standing in a moonlit copse, listening to leaves drop and birds call; the target fifty yards away, or fifty feet away, or nearer.

The hinge of a door groaned and Hackett inhaled sharply. His eyes dilated and his hand closed on the gun butt.

Paluzzi was across the clearing from him, not twenty yards away, a gun in his hand, posture nervous, hiding inside the cubicle of an old stable. Hackett, protected in heavy shadow, didn't move immediately. He stood stock still, staring impassively across the opening. Frank Paluzzi was a disappointment. Hackett remembered him and the record photo showed him as a man of fifty with greasy curled hair and a grin of success. This man looked weary and aged. Too much running, Hackett reflected wryly – too long on the game. The helicopter rattled overhead and Paluzzi looked up. Hackett took the cue. He walked slightly out of shadow. 'Paluzzi – Crime Squad. Put the gun down.'

A short hiss of breath escaped from Paluzzi's lips and Hackett thought vaguely the man had laughed. He walked forward, his hand still on the Smith & Wesson. Paluzzi stepped back fractionally.

'Crime Squad?' he said thinly. 'Someone's been looking for me, eh? Hackett?'

'That's it. Word travels.'

'Sure.'

'The gear's back. We've Abney, Robertson – the towel's in. It's over.'

'Frame of mind. Where's the heavies?'

'Put down the – '

Hackett got no further. Paluzzi dropped to his knees and fired from the hip. Hackett felt no pain, just the powerful slap on the thigh and the warmth of running blood. He fell. Paluzzi jumped up, motioned to run, thought twice of it and skipped back. He aimed the Luger. Hackett rolled over, spinning bodily into the shadow of the beech hedges. Paluzzi's gun cracked again, the shot kicking up a fistful of earth at Hackett's ear. Pebbles stung his face. Cordite filled the air. He rolled again. Paluzzi ran nearer and fired. This time the bullet slammed through the beeches, thrashing leaves all over the place. Hackett had the Smith & Wesson out. He lifted it, aimed it squarely at Paluzzi's forehead. Paluzzi seemed to be advancing, trying to shield his eyes from the glare of the moon. Hackett was listening to his own thoughts, bounding in his head like the voice of a coach. *Relax the forearms. Support the wrist. Close range, aim a fraction low. Sight and fire!* The sight was lined on Paluzzi's brow as he tightened on the trigger. Then, in a hundredth of a second, as he fired he jabbed the gun downwards. Paluzzi never got the next shot in. Hackett's bullet ripped into him, bursting through the right elbow, forcing the arm to jerk and fly in a violent spasm of movement. The Luger shot up in the air and glinted in moonlight. Paluzzi opened his mouth in a full-throated scream, grabbing the dangling arm with his left hand.

Suddenly the clearing was teeming with people. Someone jumped across Hackett's prostrate form, kicking him solidly with a heavy shoe. A woman officer he recognised as the guileless Jennie Cook charged up to Paluzzi grabbed his good arm firmly and pushed him over to face the wooden door of the stable-hut. Holding him there she began calling instructions in a manful vigorous voice. Six other officers darted onto the scene. Groaning in the darkness, someone at last uncovered Hackett and helped him to his feet. Stepping into the waning rays of moonlight, Hackett tore the material of his trouser leg away from the wound and probed roughly with the tips of his fingers. There was no metal in it and the cut was through the side of the flesh, deeply ploughed but straight. A dozen stitches and a shot of something would see it right.

Someone sidled up and slid a shoulder under his arm to support him. Soft long hair brushed his cheek, clinging to his sweat. He looked into Louise's eyes. 'You got him,' her expression seemed to say.

'I should have killed the bastard,' Hackett said, and he rubbed the tears of moisture and sweat and pain from his face.

Not long after dawn broke on a fine, crisp morning, Hackett limped into the Crime Squad office and carefully picked his way along the corridor, half-using the stick the hospital had given him, half-ignoring it.

Night shifts were just starting to change and a pleasant, luxurious silence sat heavily around the building. Only the Intelligence Bureau crackled along with the muted harmony of telex and mufax machines and the shrill counterpoint of the operations computer. Going straight to his own office he sat in his chair, leaving the blinds closed, switched on the green-shaded desk lamp and sat studying his hands. His aching limbs cried out for rest, but, before surrendering to bed he had wanted to get back into harness, to get back to his pasture and revive what had been done. For a start he had to admit to himself that the job had been concluded as cleanly as could have been hoped for in the broad sense. Of the suspected five involved in the hit, three had been, well, accounted for. The other two would still be hounded, but there was no telling whether they might ever be run to ground. The Greek junk was safety ensconced in Safelock's 'double security' vault – whatever that might be. And, more than anything, Paluzzi, the singer of the song, was in the pen. He would go down, Hackett knew, for a long time. As sole perpetrator of the crime standing trial, he would suffer doubly for his, and the team's sins. The entire focus would be on him and a good prosecutor would harp on that, amplify it, and screw him to the wall. In order to try to save himself, Paluzzi would probably shout his head off, and, with appropriate persuasion, leads to the members of the team still free might be elicited.

Hackett thought about Dink. Half his reason for coming here had been her. He would have to phone her, he knew, to tell her how his ruse had worked and how it had failed. She had given a lot, more than she had to – not to the police, but to him. What, he wondered, did she expect in return? Respectful thanks? Or something more? He shrugged. What was she entitled to? He closed his mind to the issue completely. He wasn't paid to judge those balances. His job was just to get the bastards. It didn't matter how you did it. It didn't matter who you used.

Tate looked in, his face scrubbed and sagging with sleep. He had been jostled out of bed for an hour during the high point of the round-up but had managed to sneak back. His squad had done well. No apologies were to be made to anyone, no damage had been done, no crapped-up post-mortems were called for.

'Havelock's happy,' Tate said. 'Your girlfriends did you proud. Any news on the tip-off?'

Hackett shook his head. 'We'll see when we speak to mummies and daddies.'

'Bonney's all right,' Tate said. 'We came out well. – '

'Robertson kicked it. So three of them died.'

Tate blew out his cheeks. 'So?'

'It's a pissy job.'

Tate looked at Hackett without sympathy. 'Since the beginning of this century mankind has annihilated a hundred million of his fellows one way or the other. Gas chambers, you name it.' He shrugged. 'It's a pissy life.'

After he had gone, Hackett sat and stared at the phone. What made a successful cop different from a successful villain? Measures of callousness? Maybe it was a small step from the acceptance of a terrifying statistic like Tate's to the vindication of taking a life yourself. Maybe the longer you lived in a copper's skin the harder you got and the less anything mattered. Maybe a time came when emotionally you felt nothing – no remorse, no desire for revenge, no fear, no anything. Maybe you ended up just quoting statistics and writing reports and still going to bed to sleep eight hours a night.

Phoning Dink seemed suddenly like a good idea.

THE AUTHOR

Michael Feeney Callan was born in Dublin in 1951 and was educated there. He has published stories and poetry in a wide range of periodicals and has written for radio and television. In 1977 one of his stories won the Hennessy Literary Award. He has published one previous novel, *Cinderella's Dead.*